This had to be a work of fiction for the truth to be told.

Tracee A. Hanna Presents

Andrea Jones

He Said Don't Tell

A novella.

Bella Tracee Books

This book is a work of fiction. Names, characters, places, and incidents are either products of the author's imagination or used fictionally. Any resemblance to actual events or locales or persons, living, or dead, is entirely coincidental.

ANDREA JONES
HE SAID DON'T TELL

No part of this book may be reproduced or transmitted in any form whatsoever, or by any means, electronic or mechanical, including photocopying, recording, or by any information storage and retrieval system, without permission in writing from the author and/or publisher.

For more information contact:
B. T. Books,
CS@BTBKS.com
www.BTBks.com

First Edition MAY 2019

Copyright © 2019 Andrea Jones
All rights Reserved.

ISBN-13: 978-0463592359
ISBN-13: 997-81796597653
ASIN: B07NKSFS4T
BNID: 2940161268094

INTRODUCTION

This is a tale of woe: children wronged in the most personal and vile way imaginable, blood trust broken, honor betrayed, and the aftermath of pure love gone terribly wrong. What happens when affection turns into a living hell? Who is to blame for the missed signs? What happens when family becomes the enemy? When the ties that bond begin to choke? When truth becomes too hard to face?

He Said

Don't

Tell

Andrea Jones

Bella Tracee Books

ACKNOWLEDGMENTS

I would like to thank everyone who supported me on this journey, especially those who genuinely believed me.

DEDICATION

I dedicate this book to children, teenagers, women, men who never felt like they had a voice to tell any adult, friend, family member about any verbal, mental, physical, emotional abuse going on in their life and that's its ok to speak and know you are not alone.

B. T. BOOKS
www.BTBks.com

TABLE OF CONTENTS

CHAPTER ONE
THE BEGINNINGS

The Rashond family vacationed in Florida every year. It was a time of family togetherness and joy. It was a time when everyone got along. Every member, from the youngest to the oldest, was on their best behavior; all with one single goal in mind: Have fun. The car drive to the theme park was filled with hours of jokes, sing-alongs, and laughter. For seven days and six nights, they lived in a hotel suite, a much smaller space than they were accustomed, and yet the Rashonds happily coexisted. The lines never seemed long, as they waited patiently for their turns. They rode the rides, took pictures with their favorite characters, enjoyed the theme park food, and delighted in being a typical, middle class African American family.

The vacationing Rashond family and the everyday Rashonds were very different people, a practically polar-opposite dynamic. Sometimes people, children, get lost in simply living. There were times of marital strife, instances of sibling rivalries and even periods of general discontent. The familial discord often reached the breaking point only to be snatched back from the edge of the precipice. The Rashonds were a solid family, through the good and the bad, they stayed together, that is, until the unthinkable happened to one of their own.

Aj Rashond was the first born of her parent's union, although, she was the second born to both.

She was neither her mother's nor her father's favorite child, as the mother's first-born son, Christian, took that coveted place in their mother's heart. The baby girl, Leah, captured their father's affections. From the very moment she was born, she was his beloved. In fact, she was adored by all.

Although Aj was the celebrated baby girl whose birth was the love of her parent's marriage, personified, her importance, title, and the perks of being the baby-girl only lasted for four short years, which was just enough time for resentment to build in Christian's heart. Even with the loss of her cherished position, Aj adapted with ease, as she quickly became her mother's good girl and little helper with her younger siblings. She remained her father's beloved, beautiful, first-born daughter.

Aj's father, Allen, was a police officer who advanced over the years. He was a Sergeant in the Army Reserves; which took him away from his family one weekend per month, two weeks per year. He stood five feet and nine inches tall. He was a clean cut strong and fit dark-skinned man with a military haircut. His charming wife, Mabel, was a beautiful woman who stood five inches shorter with a curvaceous build. She was a stay-at-home mom who took part-time work here and there to make ends meet. She was a devoted wife and mother who enjoyed cooking and making a good home for her family. She lovingly gave her husband four children, two daughters and two sons.

Although Allen and Mabel Rashond were happily married, not every day was filled with joy. They had five children to raise, sadly, the last one was born with a tumor. A loving household filled with children, living on a budget where sometimes bills were tight, and a child who needed so much attention and care, all created unavoidable marital strife. Having two children from previous entanglements only added tension to their relationship. There were times when things got heated; however, Allen was always quick to make up with both his wife and each one of their children. He was the kind of man who appreciated his family and would do anything to make them happy. As the years passed he grew almost famous for thoughtful gift giving and spur of the moment family trips.

One day, following a particularly trying episode in their ten-year marriage, Allen happily greeted his children in the living room after he had returned from a two-week training exercise with the Army Reserves. His wife was in the kitchen cooking dinner. Time away always gave him perspective, and his absence often cooled the waters between the two. They loved each other, and in the end nothing else mattered.

"Hello family! Mabel, I am home baby," he said jovially. "Come in here love, I've got good news."

Allen happily waited for his wife to arrive with a big grin on his face and his hand tucked behind his back. Mable popped a roast with potatoes, onions, and carrots into the oven. She washed her hands and joined her family. She smiled happily at the sight of her husband. She hugged him more affectionately at that moment than any other, as missing each other was their matrimonial plight. He presented his wife with flowers which brightened her spirits even more. He gazed into her eyes affectionately and kissed her forehead.

"Thank you, the flowers are lovely," Mable said sweetly. She tiptoed up for a most welcomed kiss. "I'm glad you're home. I've missed you honey."

"I've missed you too baby." Allen doted on his wife for a moment longer before he turned his attention to the children. "We need a vacation family. I am taking you all to the beach in Miami!" he announced.

Everyone cheered and celebrated the news. No one looked forward to the family excursions more than Aj Rashond. She knew, during the time before their trip, no one would do anything to get into trouble. She and her siblings were kinder to one another more than ever, and more forgiving. Her parents never argued. In fact, they were more accommodating and accepting of each other after his times away, just before trips, and during the vacations than any other time. It was during those days that Aj felt like she was a part of a real family, like she belonged to something wonderful.

Aj had four brothers: Christian, Andre, Alani, and Delani, and a sister, Leah, nicknamed Shorty, whom she loved. Christian was four years older, just old enough to learn to enjoy being an only child. He never truly acclimated to the new family dynamic, and his resentment often showed in his behavior. There was sibling rivalry and petty bitterness all of which was solely in his heart, as Aj loved her big brother and only wanted his love in return. As time passed and other siblings were born and came of age, she learned to refocus her love.

She was surrounded by much older boys, much younger boys and one baby sister, which left her feeling a bit left out and lonely. Aj was four years old when her little sister was born. She had already learned to amuse herself, as Christian was as close to his mother as a child could be and her father was often not at home. In addition, the baby sister got all of the attention that her brother did not demand.

As the years passed, she tried her best to be useful around the house, even though she felt more and more left out after her younger brothers were born. She often kept her younger siblings busy with games, arts, and crafts. Aj earned an allowance by doing household chores. Keeping the kitchen spotless was her specialty.

Andre and Leah were close. They were just over a year apart and bonded the moment they met. Leah was kind, gentle, and loving to her new baby brother. The two played together and often kept one another company after Alani was born. Alani was the miracle baby. He was born alive against all odds and needed a lot of medical care. There was more prayer and tension in the Rashond household after his birth than at any other time. No one knew what was going to happen, the quality of life he would have, or even if he would survive. Although everyone was as helpful, and loving has they could be, and they all wanted Alani to live, to heal, to grow; it was all in God's hands.

The Rashond family lived in a brown and white house located on the northwest side of Milwaukee, a duplex. They occupied the downstairs unit, a three-bedroom one-bathroom home. No one lived upstairs at that time, and therefore, Mr. Rashond transformed the basement into a man cave which included: two lounge chairs, a big screen television, two video game consoles, a bar, a dartboard, and a pool table. He often settled in after work as he waited for dinner. On Monday nights and on weekends he watched the game in peace. From time to time Aj joined her father. She curled up in the chair beside him and loved the time she had alone with her dad.

Aj and Marie were first cousins on her mother's side of the family. Marie was a dark skin beauty who loved to share. She had brown hair that she wore in a ponytail. The girls were very close, although they were not the same age. Growing up they did everything together. Their mothers always dressed them alike. They even went to the same school. Aj was a year ahead.

Aj went to Garfield elementary school from k4 through fifth grade. During her first year of school she met and befriended a girl named Alexa. Alexa was bright, fun, sweet and exciting. She was a child model and she sang in the church choir. Aj liked the fact that she met a friend who had a life which was very different from hers. She longed for activities that she could share with someone who was her own age. More than that, she finally had comradery.

Although Aj kept busy, she was in The Troupes, liked The Troupes meetings and activities and even looked forward to selling Troupes' cookies at different locations around town; she had no one close to her to share the experience with, as it was a competition. She competed with all that she was and was often the top salesperson in her group. Aj played basketball, and she was fond of being a part of a team, although she never really made friends with any of her team members. There was no adverse reason for that fact, other than not clicking with one of the girls over another. Aj preferred personal, compelling reasons for being a friend.

Alexa, who was not in The Troupe nor did she play basketball, provided the companionship Aj sought. Alexa's life was very different from Aj's, which broadened her childhood experiences. As their friendship grew, the girls spent the night at each other's houses on alternate weekends. Although Aj was surrounded by family, having a best friend made her feel less alone. As the years passed, the girls were almost inseparable until sixth grade when Alexa went to a different middle school. Aj and Alexa valued their friendship and therefore the sleepovers continued.

Aj attended Jackie Robinson middle school for sixth, seventh, and eighth grade. While the middle school was located across the street from a police station, the students would still get into fights. Aj never cared about school clicks or popularity. Her quiet nature kept her out of trouble. Granted, she felt alone without Alexa and pretty much kept to herself, however, before long she met a pair of twins Layla and Paula, and the three of them became fast friends. The twins were welcoming, sociable, loyal, and never argued. Aj and the twins spent a lot of time together, confided in one another and shared each-others hopes for the future. They did a lot of after school activities together. They were on the drill team and in the ceramics club.

Aj tried a lot of afterschool activities, anything to keep busy, and anything to feel less forlorn. She loved the creativity of ceramics. She enjoyed molding the clay into something beautiful. She created little African American figurines and watched on happily as the teacher placed it in the kiln to harden. Once it was finished, Aj, Layla, and Paula painted them. They were a trio of very talented young artists, so much so the school created a display of their ceramic works of art for all to enjoy. Aj felt proud to have her work exhibited. It gave her a sense of accomplishment. In fact, she made an African American Christmas Angel for her family's tree one year, when she was nine years old.

Christmas nineteen ninety-seven was one to remember. The Rashond family hosted a party for friends and family. The house was perfectly clean and decorated with Aj's angel at the top of the tree for all to see. She and every member of her family were dressed elegantly for the occasion. As the guests arrived and the party gained life, Aj gushed with pride at the many complements her angel received, the image of which was modeled after her lovely mother.

An hour after the last guest had arrived, Nancy, Aj's maternal aunt, a license practical nurse, arrived with her fiancé, Ron, in tow. She was tall and skinny with long hair. She craved attention and openly competed against any, and all females, especially her sister, Mable, who never cared.

"Hey y'all!" Nancy bellowed, as she loved making an entrance and it showed at every event. She often dressed as if she was a headliner in Las Vegas: over the top makeup, gaudy clothes, and fetish type high heel shoes. No matter the occasion, family picnic, trip to the grocery store or a Christmas party, she was in character and costume. The children called, Aunt Nancy, the one woman show. She never failed to disappoint. Most people felt sorry for her fiancé because Nancy was sue-happy, clingy, and controlling.

Ron was a warehouse worker who wanted to be a firefighter; however, his wife would not allow it. He had a strong muscular build. He was six feet tall, very fit, and smiled all of the time. He always wore tight pants and a shirt that was two sizes too small. He often casually flexed his muscles even when he stood alone. He wore dark sunglasses morning, noon, and night; both indoors and out, no matter the season or occasion. His eyes were usually covered. No one knew exactly why, although some suspected it was to hide his embarrassment. Or maybe it was so he could roll his eyes at Nancy's shenanigans without getting cussed out. No one quite understood his attraction to Nancy. Although she was not an unattractive woman, her personality made her difficult to bear for most people, except for Ron. He seemed to have patience for her that no other person on the earth could muster.

While Nancy floated through the party and socialized with the adults, all the while, Ron played with the children. He picked the girls up and twirl them around one by one. He divided the change in his pocket amongst the children, however, he always ran out of coins when it was Aj's turn, as he coincidentally greeted her dead last every time, accidentally on purpose. As he approached her, his smile brightened. He hunched down and scooped her up in his arms. He spun her around until she giggled with glee. When he placed her back on her feet, she was a little dizzy. He held her in his arms until she regained her equilibrium.

"How's my pretty girl?" asked Ron.

Aj giggled a little more, as she was shy and did not know what to say. "Merry Christmas Ron," she finally muttered.

"Merry Christmas baby," Ron replied as he bent down before her. "I have a little something for you."

"Really," asked Aj as she beamed up at him.

Ron turned out his front pockets one by one. Aj saw each pocket was empty. She shifted from one foot to the other nervously. She tried her level best to hide her disappointment. Ron reached in his last pock, the back pocket on the right, and retrieved his wallet. There was plenty of money inside.

"I don't have any change to give you my beauty, however, I do have something better," he stated triumphantly as he pulled several bills out of his billfold. "Hold out your hand."

Aj did as instructed. Her excitement could not be contained. She bounced in her toes and grinned happily. One by one Ron placed ten dollars in her palm. He covered her hand with his and closed them both. He kissed her cheek, stood up, and walked away. Aj skipped ways happily gripping her spoils. She scampered off to her room and hid the money in her special place. She returned to the party and spotted Ron who stood alone facing her direction. He smiled at her, or so it seemed, as he always smiled. She gave him a quick wave and smile before she joined the other children, happy in the knowledge that she was finally someone's favorite.

"How much did you get Aj?" Marie asked.

"Enough for me to get candy and soda after school for a month," Aj said as she beamed with joy. "What about you Marie? How much did he give you?"

"I only got a dollar. I guess you really are his favorite."

"Aunt Nancy is at it again," Christian stated to the kids' group as he pointed her out. Every child looked over to her.

Nancy was in full form. She was flamboyant and laughed too loud. She danced around from person to person garnering as much attention as she could muster. She finally landed before her sister and brother-in-law, who stood together with drinks in their hands watching on with idle curiosity. She struck a pose and waited. Allen and Mabel looked at each other. His expression clearly stated, your sister, and her gaze replied; I know baby.

"Merry Christmas Nancy," Allen greeted Nancy cordially as she smiled brazenly into his eyes.

"Merry Christmas dear sister," Mabel chimed in.

Nancy never acknowledged her sister, as she was transfixed on her brother-in-law. "Merry Christmas," Nancy crooned as she went in for a hug which, to her chagrin, Allen sidestepped with a handshake. Mabel smiled to herself satisfied with her husband's response. Nancy turned her attention to her sister. "I see you have lost some of the baby weight, congratulations," her false tone was clear.

Before Mabel could reply her husband interjected, "She is absolutely lovely just as she is."

Allen looked at his wife lovingly and kissed her cheek. She peered into his eyes and tiptoed up for a real kiss. In that moment, defeated, Nancy simply walked away. Allen and Mabel gazed at each other and laughed as they often did when it came to Nancy carrying on foolishly. The children, after they witnessed the scene unfold, laughed as well.

Coco, Mabel's little sister, walked over after the coast was clear. She and her sister looked into each other's eyes and snickered under their breath. Seeing that his wife was in good hands Allen took his leave. Coco and Mabel shared a drink as they watch their sister Nancy work the party. They never talked about her behind her back, as neither one of them wanted to be cruel.

As the party progressed, Nancy floated from man to man; all the while Ron appeared to enjoy the music nonchalantly. She completely ignored her fiancé and yet seemed to keep him close by. Although he stayed near her, he never seemed to look her way. His head was always pointed in any direction but hers. Little did anyone know, Ron kept watch on Aj, her every move, her every expression, he was transfixed by her beauty.

Aj picked up her baby brother and grabbed her baby sister by the hand. Christian picked up Andre and they went down the hall to the bedrooms. Aj and Christian put their younger sibling to bed before they returned to the party. They were the only children who were awake as their cousins found places to sleep on the couch and floor of the living room. The party moved to the basement where the guests amused themselves with conversation, darts, and pool. Mabel and Coco busied themselves bringing snacks and drinks down for the guests. Nancy chose that moment to interact with Allen once again, as he stood alone.

"Allen, this is the best Christmas party I've been to in years," Nancy stated with a little too much excitement, as she grabbed him by the arm.

"Thank you," Allen replied. He pulled away and busied himself with priming the beer keg.

Christian and Aj looked on from a corner in the room. They kept quiet as they did not want to be sent to bed. The older brother looked at his sister and she looked him. It was dually understood that Aunt Nancy was nothing but trouble.

"Never be that kind of woman Aj," Christian stated emphatically.

"I never will," Aj replied in honest.

"She is the type of woman who would ruin a family and not care."

"I know, and I never want to be like her."

Mabel retuned to the party and took her place next to her husband, after which, Nancy finally stood by Ron's side. The children continued to look on.

"She only wants Ron when there is no other choice," Aj stated boldly.

"Well, she cannot have Dad." Christian replied immediately.

"No, she cannot," Aj agreed instantly.

The party continued into the night. Guests played pool, cards and darts. They danced to R&B music, talked, laughed, and nibbled on the snacks. As the party fizzed Christian and Aj slipped off to bed. People gathered their coats and children in their arms and bode the hosts good night. Nancy and Ron were the last gusts to leave.

"This was a nice little Christmas party Mabel," Nancy stated dismissively.

"Thank you?" Mabel replied.

"My wife always hosts the perfect party," Allen interjected as he snaked his arm around his wife. He kissed the side of her head before she smiled at

Nancy. Nancy grabbed Ron's arm and pulled him close. He moved like a puppet and stood by her side. There was no show of affection, just duty.

"I would like to announce our wedding date," Nancy said with flair. "Our wedding will be in about six months… from today." She looked at Allen and continued, "I will no longer be a free woman."

"Congratulations to you both," Allen said as he looked at Ron sympathetically.

Nancy pushed her sister aside as she stole a hug from Allen, who rolled his eyes in total disbelief. His arms remained at his sides. She lingered with her arms wrapped around him until he finally returned her embrace. He touched her as lightly as humanly possible, as he patted her back and almost instantly ended the hug. Allen stepped away from Nancy and enveloped his wife lovingly in his embrace.

"We are happy for you both Nancy," Mabel said with a smile.

"Congrats Ron, it has been a long time coming, high school sweethearts, nice." Allen added, "Let me get your coats."

The next morning each member of the Rashond family entered the kitchen one by one and took a seat at the table for breakfast. Mabel and Christian busied themselves making blueberry pancakes, bacon, and eggs. Allen helped Alani into his highchair. Mabel plated the pancakes and eggs before she turned to her family and smiled. Just as she took her seat, Christian placed a plate of bacon in the center of the table.

"I'm ready to eat," Christian announced after Allen blessed the food.

"This bacon is burnt," Aj complained and then spit it out.

"That's the way I like it," Christian replied.

Alani took a bite of bacon and spit it out. "Burnt," he said.

The children laughed. Mabel and Allen looked at from one to the other. Tears welled up in Mabel's eyes as she slowly stood and picked Alani up. She held him tight.

"Yes, burnt. Say it again... burnt." Mabel kissed her baby boy over and over again. She laughed and cried. "Allen, after all of these years, he said his first word. Burnt..."

CHAPTER TWO
FIRST SIGNS

Nineteen ninety-eight was a year that would change lives forever. Mabel and Allen were overjoyed at the progress Alani made, as no one thought he would ever speak. While the months passed, his speech developed from single words into full and complete sentences. The miracle of his recovery brought the Rashond family closer together. Allen retired from the military. As his family congealed, he longed to spend more time at home being a husband and father. Christian was a freshman in high school, and he took up an interest in becoming a chef. Aj was in middle school where she blossomed into a responsible young lady, so much so, her aunt Nancy asked her to be an usher in her wedding. She gladly agreed, if Marie could be one too.

Nancy and Ron were married in a church ceremony on a sunny afternoon in July. Summer had been kind in Milwaukee that year. The warm breezed and cooling rains resembled more of a Springtime feeling. The sky was clear and sunny as people entered the church, which was on the corner of Fond du Lac and North Avenue. Aj was proud to be included in such a joyous day. She stood with her back straight, dressed in white: skirt, blouse, stockings, gloves and shoes. Marie stood opposite Aj, the mirror image. The young ladies were posted at the grand mahogany double doors just beyond the vestibule. Their hearts filled with excitement every time they greeted the attendees. Aj and Marie smiled happily as they dutifully showed each guest to their seats.

It was a super nice wedding. Their colors were red and white. The groomsmen were dressed in white suites with red cummerbunds, the bridesmaids wore passion red long halter-top dresses, the church was filled with red roses and white lilies and the bride wore white. Her gown was long sleeved and beaded with a long train and a dramatic v-bodice. The bride was veiled as she walked down the aisle. The ceremony only lasted about an hour, after that everyone hung round to take pictures with the wedding party outside of the church.

Aj stood alone, out of the way, as she patiently waited for her turn to come and go. She watched on contentedly at the splendor. It was the groom's men turn to pose with the bride and groom. The bride's maids gathered on the lawn in front of Aj.

"Would it have killed her to wear a bra?" Aj overheard a bride's maid comment.

"No pushup bra in Wisconsin could have lifted those banana peels," another lady replied.

"Banana peels?"

"Take a look and tell me if I'm wrong."

"Ha! You're right, so flat."

The ladies giggled. Aj laughed to herself and walked away to get a better view. Once she was settled at a comfortable distance she watched on. That was the moment she saw Ron. She had not recalled him ever being without his sunglasses before, and therefore she observed with idle curiosity. Uncle Ron has a nice ring to it. I'm his favorite and he is my uncle now. Aj smiled and he caught her gaze.

Ron stared at Aj for the longest moment. The photographer had to call out to him a few times to get his attention back. The entire wedding party was called over to the church steps for a group photo. Aj happily took her place and smiled her brightest. Once the bride's maids and groomsmen photos were taken, they excused themselves to the reception hall. The only people left at the church were family. Aj. Marie, and Christian followed their Aunt Coco into the church and gathered all of the flowers. Nancy insisted on last minute photos surrounded by bouquets.

Aj exited the church, just after Marie, with her arms filled to the max with roses. Ron's eyes locked on her immediately. Uncle Ron has been looking at me so hard today, Aj thought. As of today, we are family. Today should be the happiest day for everyone, but this doesn't feel right. He did not blink, never once. She looked down in shame. Did I do something wrong, am I in trouble? Aj reflected on her duties as an usher, which she was confident she performed perfectly. When she looked up again, her new Uncle Ron's gaze was focused on her still. Why is he staring at me like that, she asked herself before she walked away. Aj went to the parking lot and rested on the back of her parents' car.

Once the photo session was over, everyone preceded to the wedding reception, where both sides of the family met, some for the very first time, and mingled. They ate delicious food catered by a top-notch soul food restaurant in Milwaukee, although the bride and groom were on a budget, Nancy insisted on the best. The wedding feast included: baked chicken, mashed potatoes, string beans and a dinner roll, simple yet delicious. After dinner came the toasts.

"To my beloved sister on her wedding day..." Mabel began as she hoisted her champagne glass to the crowd, "May you finally find the happiness that you so deserve."

Everyone cheered and toasted. The DJ chose that moment to play an old school R&B ballot to which the bride and groom shared their first dance. There were many toast and dances before the party found its legs and took on a life of its own.

During the fast songs and group dances the children felt comfortable enough to finally partake. The traditional line dance stepping, where everyone came out on the dance floor at once and followed steps, was Aj's favorite. It was in those moments when she and her cousins shined. They were on the dance floor dancing to all the 90's line jams every chance they got. They were happy, all of the children, from both sides, felt as if they were a part of something spectacular, the joining of two families.

It was that night that Aj's feelings for Ron changed. There was something about him that crept her out. He stared at her for long periods of time that night while she danced. She caught him time and time again. I mean who stares that long without blinking, Aj mused. She tried her best to escape his ogling. She walked away every time she caught him staring.

The night progressed. It seems as though Uncle Ron is following me around, Aj thought. Every time I go to get something to eat or drink, he is magically standing there beside me or behind me. However, she had her doubts. Maybe he could just have been thirsty and hungry too, she guessed. Aj put her misgiving out of her mind.

Not too long after the wedding Aj and her cousin Marie went by their Aunt Nancy's house to spend the night, at their Aunt's request. It was August and the cousins, to both of their delights, finally attended the same school again. They ate lunch together every day. Marie smiled as she spotted Aj sitting at their regular table from the lunch line. Aj smiled and she waited for Marie to join her.

"Did you remember to bring your overnight bag?" Marie asked after she took a seat across from Aj.

"Yes, I sure did," Aj replied with a grin. She stole one of Marie's tortilla chips. "I should've got some nachos."

"It's not too late," Marie replied as she moved her plate closer to herself.

"I'm good. My pizza is fine. Aunt Nancy is making fried chicken with macaroni and cheese tonight. I'm leaving plenty of room for dinner."

"Me too, that's why I got the nachos."

"Right, right, so what game do you want to play first?"

"I don't know, I'll think about it and tell you after school. What about you?"

"Monopoly of course, I will take all of your money."

"That's the longest game ever, it takes all night to play."

"Yeah, but that's my game though. We can play Checkers before dinner and Monopoly after."

"Sounds like a plan…"

Aj and Marie met after school. Together they walked to their aunt's house. Nancy and Ron lived in a two-bedroom apartment not far from their school.

They kept plenty of board games. Aj and Marie played Checkers and Connect Four while they waited for Nancy to cook dinner. Ron sat with their four-year-old daughter, their first-born daughter, Niyah, on his lap and watched the girls.

After dinner Nancy put Niyah to bed, she joined Aj, Marie, and Ron in a game of Monopoly. They had the best of times, as they played vigorously against each other, and everyone played to win. About mid-way through the game Nancy left the room. She checked on her daughter who was sleeping peacefully. Marie chose that moment to excuse herself to the bathroom, which left Aj and Ron alone together. Aj busied herself counting her money. She was happy with herself. She did quite well at that point in the game.

"Marie needs to hurry up, I can't hold it any longer," Aj announced urgently as she stood up. "I'll be right back Uncle Ron."

Aj walked past Ron, Nancy's husband, and he said just loud enough for her ears only, "Make sure you were those shorts again."

Shocked, her head snapped towards him. Her eyes bugged, as she glared in disgust. The way he smiled at her, sickened her instantly. Aj stumbled over her feet while she attempted to keep moving, thankfully, she did not fall. She turned forward and exited the room as quickly as possible. On her way out, she passed Nancy and Marie on their way back in.

Everything that Aj felt at the wedding came flooding back. She scurried off to the bathroom. She was mortified and wanted to cry. She wanted to tell her aunt; however, she did not know how. She looked in the bathroom mirror and wondered: What have I done wrong to garner a grown man's attention? Why would a grown man say that to me, thinking it is normal? He is supposed to be my uncle. A tear escaped her eyes and she swiftly wiped it away.

Aj wore a typical summer short set. Her shorts were green with small watermelon print and her shirt had one matching larger watermelon print centered on the front. She was eleven years old, a child, an innocent. She quickly used the bathroom and washed her hands. She splashed cold water on her face and then dried off. It's nothing, she thought, he just likes my shorts. They're cute. He just said it wrong.

Aj rejoined the game. The joy of the evening was lost to her. Every time she looked up, she caught Ron staring at her. She grew more and more uncomfortable. He slid his sunglasses on, although it was nighttime, and they were in the house. Even so, Aj could feel his eyes on her. Once the game was over, Aj and Marie carefully packed up the pieces. Marie returned the game to the shelf. Nancy went and checked on the baby again. In her absence, Aj packed up the Connect Four game as quickly as she could muster, as she did not want to be left behind with Ron ever again. Ron approached her as she scooped the game into her arms and tried to leave the room.

"Remember, what happens in this house stays in this house," Ron said unequivocally.

Aj, made her way past Ron just as Marie returned. Nancy peeked in the room and walked pass to the backroom. Aj grabbed Marie by the hand and turned her around. She pulled her along as she kept it moving.

"Come with me to put these games away. I don't want to stack them up wrong and the all fall over," Aj said.

"Yeah, you don't want that to happen," Marie chuckled as she spoke.

When the girls returned to the living room Nancy announced, "It is time for bed. It is getting late and you two have to get up early in the morning."

"Yes ma'am," the girls said together.

"Come on Ron, let these girls get some sleep."

Ron followed Nancy out of the room. Aj and Marie made a sheet fort and rolled out their sleeping bags inside. They climbed in and zipped themselves up. The young girls whispered to each other until they drifted off to sleep.

The following morning, Aj woke up, took a bath, brushed her teeth, and got dressed. She was all too ready to go back home and get Marie to safety. The Rashond family did not live too far from Nancy's house, as it was only a ten-minute walk away. She and Marie thanked their aunt and uncle for having them over. They gathered their book bags and headed out, however Ron stopped them at the door just long enough to say a creepy goodbye.

Aj played Ron's haunting words over and over again in her mind on the walk home. She was lost in thought, I don't want to cause any trouble, so I am not going to tell Aunt Nancy, and after all, they just got married. I do know one thing, I am never going back there ever again, she decided.

"What's wrong Aj?" Marie asked, worried. "You've been acting weird all morning."

"Nothing," Aj smiled at her cousin. She skipped and matched Marie's steps. "I think I'm too old to be going over to Aunt Nancy's to spend the night."

"Didn't you have fun? I know I did."

"Yeah, but we can have fun without being there. My daddy has a pool table and a dart board. We can save our money and get some more board games."

"True. And we can camp out in the backyard instead of in the living room."

"Exactly!"

Aj never went back to spend the night at Nancy's and Ron's apartment, and neither did Marie. Aj just knew she would be safe at home; after all she was a cop's daughter. No one would be stupid enough to come into a cop's home and harm a cop's daughter under a cop's roof. Little did she know how far from the truth the one truth she held self-evident would be.

As time passed the Rashond house became the spot. Allen and Mabel hosted almost every holiday party known to Americans. Aj was forced to see Ron again and again, however she kept her distance. In fact, there was never a time when Nancy dropped by that Ron was not with her. It was as if they were stuck together like glue, and Aj had to accept that fact, as she never saw one without the other.

Occasion after occasion: Labor Day, Columbus Day, Veteran's Day, Thanksgiving, and Christmas, Aj withdrew from her family. She wore tomboyish baggy clothes whenever she knew Nancy and Ron were going to visit. Nancy and Ron were visiting more and more with each passing month, and not only on occasions. They would stop by with their daughter, Niyah, out of the blue. Ron always carried her in and put her down to play.

Aj never smiled at Ron ever again. She never hugged him either, at least not voluntarily. She watched on with disgust as the other children threw themselves into his arms and squealed as he spun them around. She eyed Ron suspiciously as he gave the girls more money than the boys. With everything that she was, Aj wanted to warn all of the girls away from Ron.

She often wondered: How can I protect my little sister and cousins without starting trouble? Who would believe me? This man who is married to my aunt is watching me all of the time. He keeps catching me alone and touching and rubbing on me calling it a hug.

☙

New Year's Day came and went, and Martin Luther King Day had finally arrived. It was a joyous day for the Rashond family as they celebrated the life and times of Martin Luther King Jr., and the civil rights movement. The extended family was over for the Martin Luther King Day Family barbeque.

Nancy was in the living room talking with the ladies. All of the men were downstairs in the basement. They enjoyed the treasures of Allen's man cave, all that is except for Ron. He lurked around upstairs. He stood with his dark shades on, in the space between where the living room, basement, and children's rooms met. He seemingly peeked in on his daughter for time to time, however he never joined in any adult activities or conversations.

"Aj," Mabel called out.

"Yes ma'am," Aj answered immediately as she sprung to her feet. She entered the living room. "Yes ma'am?"

"Baby, will you do the dishes right now? The kitchen is getting out of control."

"Yes ma'am."

Mabel smiled lovingly at Aj. She returned her mother's smile before she headed into the kitchen. Doing the dishes was part of her chores, and Aj always did what was expected of her. Aj looked around the kitchen and took a deep breath. Between cooking and the first round of food service, the kitchen had gotten more than a little out of sorts. No matter, she thought as she dove right in, I'll have this cleaned up in no time.

"Hey Nancy baby, I'm going downstairs with the fellas for a few minutes," Ron all but asked, as his tone sought approval.

"Okay but don't be too long," Nancy ordered.

Ron dropped in on Aj in the kitchen, on the way to the basement. He stood behind his wife's niece, who felt she was no longer alone. He placed his hands on her waist and pressed up against her for a quick squeeze. When she turned around however, Ron was gone. She shook her head scornfully and said, "This has got to stop." This is so wrong, she thought as she returned to her task, that is not how a grown man should touch a child.

Aj's parents were in the living room along with other family members when Aj finished the dishes. Everyone was engrossed in a discussion about the pros and cons of marching for different causes and the benefits of peaceful resistance instead of violence.

Aj listened carefully as she was determined to fight the injustices that Ron inflicted upon her.

"What do you do," Aj started timidly, "when you are forced to keep quiet?" She found her voice as she continued, "When violence will only make you lose everything, how can you make someone…" Aj looked directly at Ron and pressed on, "stop?"

Nancy followed Aj's gaze, no one else did. When Aj returned her attention to the rest of her family she noticed Nancy get up and go stand by her husband. Aj scoffed in disgust. Oh, so now you want to be all hugged up and lovey-dovey with your wife after you had your stuff pressed up against my back? Ron is so gross.

"Aj did you hear me?" Coco asked.

"No ma'am. I'm sorry, what did you say?" Aj replied as she looked to her aunt for some guidance.

"I said, history teaches us that you can never keep injustices quiet forever. There always comes a time when the wronged party gets fed up and seeks justice. Some things take longer than others, however in the end it is always worth it when you stand up for yourself."

"Thank you, Aunt Coco," Aj said with a hug.

Aj did not know what to do however she knew she must do something. She was bound and determined to expose Ron for the creeper that he was. Just as Aj looked over at Ron, Nancy yelled out, "We need some music! This is supposed to be a party!" and before long the discussion was lost to the music.

CHAPTER THREE
FALSE SENSE OF COMFORT

Aj avoided Ron like the plague. No matter what the occasion and no matter whose house at which the party was held, Aj sought to protect herself. It was fairly easy to tell when Ron and Nancy arrived at any family function as Nancy loved nothing more than to announce her own arrival. She announced everything that she did before she did it and therefore tracking her was super simple. She also concluded with, come on baby, whenever she wanted Ron to accompany her. The devil was in the details, to discern when Ron was on the move, alone.

Ron wore shoes that made a big squishy squeaky sound as the ball of his foot rolled forward and rounded out each step. Aj knew the sound well. She forced herself to learn it and to recognize it above all else, and therefore, she always listened for Ron's footsteps, no matter whose company or what activities she might have otherwise enjoyed. She decided the best way to save herself was to steer clear of her Aunt Nancy's husband all together.

Aj attended a party at Lynn's house in celebration of Marie's eleventh birthday. The two first cousins dressed alike, as they usually did. They wore matching pink and yellow flowered capri pants with flowered long-sleeved cashmere sweaters, Aj wore the yellow and Marie wore the pink. Aj wore her hair down in a stylish wrap, while Marie's head was filled with bouncy curls. The birthday party was well on its way when Nancy and Ron arrived.

"Hey y'all," Nancy announced loudly.

A chill went up Aj's spine. She slowly turned and faced her aunt but refused to allow her gaze to settle on Ron. She stood still as Marie ran over to her aunt and uncle. Ron scooped Marie up and twirled her around.

"Happy birthday," he said as she giggled.

"Thank you, Uncle Ron," Marie replied with a smile.

Ron put her down and reached into his pocket. He smiled at her has he retrieved his wallet and peered inside. He whipped out a crispy ten-dollar bill and gave it to her. She jumped with joy and threw her arms around him. He picked her up and spun her around again. When he placed her back on her feet, she thanked him once more and ran back to Aj. Immediately, Marie showed off her spoils.

"Look Aj, Uncle Ron gave me ten dollars," Marie exclaimed.

"Let's go to the penny candy store tomorrow," Aj said genuinely happy for her cousin.

"Okay," Marie agreed cheerfully. "You always share with me, it's my turn to share with you."

The whole time the cousins talked Ron crept towards them. He would stop intermittently and greet different family members as he went. Before Aj knew it, he was upon her. She looked up shocked and a little bit frightened as she did not hear him coming. The first thing she noticed was his smile and the sunglasses that he wore almost all of the time. Aj turned to leave however she was stopped by his words.

"Where's my hug at?" asked Ron.

When she turned back around Nancy was standing next to him. Aj stood frozen in that moment. What do I do now, she asked herself, with everyone staring at me? I don't want that man putting his hands on me again.

"Quit acting stuck up Aj, and give your Uncle Ron a hug," Nancy stated loud enough for all to hear.

Aj did not move. Her stare was unfriendly as she thought: Your husband is a creeper Aunt Nancy, sneaking up from behind me kissing my neck every chance he gets. He is not my uncle!

"What? You too good now?" Nancy persisted.

I don't want to get in trouble for acting funny. I know I must do what was expected of me and yet everything in me wants to run away and save myself. Aj reluctantly stepped forward, and Ron gave her a quick friendly hug and moved on.

Even still, Aj felt dirty. Her brow furrowed as she was left standing there lost in thought. I cannot believe I had too… No, I was forced to hug Ron by my own family. Don't they realize when a child does not want to be touched by an adult, or any person they used to love, something has gone terribly wrong?

Marie noticed Aj the change in right away. She made her way over to her cousin and smiled, a smile which Aj automatically returned. Marie motioned for Aj to follow her to her room. Once they were alone Marie closed the door.

"What's wrong Aj? Don't you like Uncle Ron anymore?"

"It's nothing Marie," Aj assured. "Don't worry about it."

"Why didn't he give you any money? You are his favorite."

"It's your birthday, not mine. Come on Marie, let's get some chips and soda," Aj said. She opened Marie's bedroom door and walked towards the kitchen.

"Okay," Marie replied merrily and followed.

As the party progressed Aj's mood lightened. She actively listened for the creaky squeak of Ron's shoes, as she did not want to face a second encounter. The moment she heard Ron approach her direction she was on the move. In fact, she became a master at escaping his attentions.

☙

Aj needed money. Gone were the days when she had plenty of cash to stop by the penny candy store every day after school with Marie. She missed having her own means. She and her siblings collected cans to earn a few dollars and some change, but it was not enough for her. She longed to buy chips and juice and her favorite treats and therefore she decided to get a job.

Aj applied to work at the local burger joint and to her happy surprise they hired her at the tender age of twelve. Her parents admired her tenacity. She worked for an hour and a half after school and a full eight-hour shift on weekends, as she was bound and determined to have her own money and to purchase her own things.

Once Aj received her first paycheck her father, took her to the bank to set up her first account. She was so proud standing there next to him in the line and even more so once she received her paperwork and it was official. Aj deposited her first paycheck and smiled up at her dad.

"I'm proud of you baby girl," Allen said as they exited the bank. He reached his hand out to her.

"Thank you, Daddy," replied Aj as she took his hand and skipped along beside him all the way to the car.

One day after work Aj walked into the kitchen while Mabel prepared dinner. Aj felt a little shy at first however her confidence returned quickly. She needed to talk to her mother.

"Hey Ma," Aj greeted her mother with ease.

"What girl," Mabel replied as she often did. She continued with her tasks.

"I need a bra."

Mabel stopped cold. She turned and faced Aj, her eyes were a little sad as she looked her daughter over. She wiped her hands on the kitchen towel and took a seat at the table. Aj joined her.

"No Aj, it's not time yet," Mabel said emphatically, reluctant to acknowledge that her little girl was developing into a young lady.

"I just want to be properly covered Ma," Aj argued.

"You don't need one girl. You aren't there yet."

"Yes ma'am," Aj responded before she took her leave.

Mabel watched her go. A pang of melancholy touched her heart as her daughter exited the kitchen. She sat for a moment longer before she rose and continued with dinner.

The next weekend, after work, Aj was excited to use her money debit card for the very first time. She called Marie. It was the weekend that the cousins spent the night at Coco's house with their cousin Melanie. Coco was the favorite aunt. All of the children always felt welcome at her house and she did the girls hair in the newest styles. Melanie, Coco's daughter, was a sweet seven-year-old little girl who loved to play with dolls and her cousins.

"Hey Marie," Aj greeted her cousin happily.

"What's up Aj? Are you on your way over to Aunt Coco's house?"

"I was thinking we could go to the mall first. You want to meet me?"

"Yeah," Marie replied overjoyed. "Let me ask my mom first."

"Okay."

Aj held the phone. She overheard Marie ask her mother if it was okay to go to the mall. Lynn agreed. She also heard Marie ask her mother for some money. Aj smiled as she thought, I earned my own money. She did not want to be a burden to her parents and the fact that she did not have to ask for cash was more than just a relief. Aj was pleased with her accomplishments.

Before long the cousins were on their way. They went from store to store perusing. Aj's very first purchase was a bra. After shopping at the mall, Aj invited Marie to go to the movie theater. Aj happily paid for the tickets, popcorn, soda, and candy. The cousins enjoyed their evening together, two young ladies out on the town. Aj delighted in being self-sufficient, as she spent her money on the things that she needed and treated her cousin. She knew, as long as she had her own money, she did not need to ask for anything.

&

Just before spring, the sun rose earlier and higher in the sky, the days grew longer, and the snow in Milwaukee began to melt. It was Troupes Cookie season. Aj spent as much time as she could selling cookies. In fact, she was the top salesperson in her troupe. Aj sold cookies to the students, teachers, and parents at school, to her co-workers and customers at work, to the ladies at church, and at the grocery store with other troupe members. Her father helped her sell cookies as well. He came home with a sheet filled with orders from his fellow officers.

Aj was beyond happy when her father presented her with the sales sheet Friday night after dinner. She thanked him and gave him a big hug before she scampered off to her room. She sat on her bed and counted up the orders. With these sales, Aj thought, I can just stay home tomorrow night.

The next morning, after Aj finished up washing the dishes she sat in her room on the floor bagging up the cookie orders and carefully checking her list. She made a list of the cookies that she needed from her troupe leader. Once she completed her task, she called her troupe leader and informed her that she would not be in attendance at the grocery store that evening. Aj went to work at the burger shop and returned home just after six pm. She went to her room, changed out of her uniform, and relaxed. Before long the doorbell rang. Mabel answered the door.

"Hey y'all!" bellowed Nancy as she entered the house, "We stopped by to see what y'all are up to tonight."

Ron, sunglasses firmly in place, entered behind his wife carrying Niyah. He put the baby down so she could go play. His shoes screeched and creaked as he stepped further into the house. He wore tight blue slacks and a turtleneck sweater which stretched so thinly over his torso every knit loop stitch laid flat. He carried a six pack of beer in one hand, with a super large bag of cheesy corn curls, and a satisfied smile on his face, like he had finally arrived.

Meanwhile, Aj was in her room lying on her bed talking on the phone to Alexa, her friend from school. The moment she heard Nancy's voice, Aj leapt to her feet. "Sorry, I gotta go," Aj said abruptly and then hung up the phone. She threw the phone onto her bed, grabbed her chic tote, and made a mad dash for the door.

"Hi," Aj said greeted Nancy and Ron on the run. "Ma, I have a Troupe meeting today and I'm running late," she said as she rushed past her mother and continued on out the front door which Mabel had yet to close. "It's our last week of selling cookies. Okay bye," Aj finished as she sped down the walkway.

"That girl," Mabel said. She watched her daughter go for a moment before she slowly closed the door and turned her attention to her niece and all but sang in her sweetest voice, "Niyah… Hi, you want a cookie baby."

❧

A week later, Mabel hustled and bustled about town, from the grocery store to the party store to the liquor store in preparation for her husband's surprise birthday party. She had invited friends, family, and Allen's co-workers over to the house, weeks in advance. Mabel woke up bright and early that morning. She kissed her husband awake.

"Happy birthday bae," she said.

"Thank you bae, and I know exactly what I want for my birthday," Allen replied.

Later that morning, after breakfast, Mabel sent her husband across town to the hardware store. The moment he kissed his wife goodbye and the front door close behind him, Mabel and her children ran down the stairs to the basement. Mabel and Christian hung the crepe streamers while Aj helped Leah, Andre, and Alani blow up balloons. They had the Allen's man cave looking festive in no time at all.

The surprise birthday party went off without a hitch. Allen was truly surprised, and his heart was filled with joy. He took his wife into his arms and kissed her soundly. Everyone cheered. About an hour later, once the party was in full swing, Nancy and Ron made their appearances.

"Hey y'all," Nancy called out in her usual fashion. Ron stood next to her, holding their daughter in his arms, dressed in tight brown slacks and a skintight long-sleeved beige shirt. He put her down as the children ran over and greeted them. Aj looked on in disgust as Ron twirled the girls around. She often wondered why his sunglasses never flew off with all of that spinning around he did. The party continued on, and as it did Aj did her level best to keep away from Ron.

After Allen's birthday party, Nancy and Ron made popping in a regular thing. As time passed, Ron seemed to become Allen's new best friend. He would find reasons to stop by with his wife and child in tow. Although he claimed to be in the Rashond's home to watch the game on the big screen, play pool, or video games downstairs in the man cave, he was often upstairs walking around alone. He would excuse himself to the bathroom so often one might think he had a prostate disorder. He went upstairs to check on his wife and daughter. He said he needed a snack. Any excuse would do.

Every time Ron ascended the stairs he went in search for Aj, and every time she heard him coming she made sure she was not by herself. Even when she had to wash the dishes, she talked one of her siblings into keeping her company, she bribed them with candy. From the moment Ron and Nancy entered, Aj went on full alert and went into protective mode. Everyday Ron was in the Rashond house, Aj saw him. He always loomed at the entrance of whatever room she occupied until he garnered her attention.

Aj sat on the floor in her bedroom one early evening. She was determined to get her homework completed before she went to work. At the same time, she helped her sister with her math assignment. Leah was eight years old, in third grade, with a sweet as pie disposition. She lay on her stomach stretched out next to Aj. Pencil in hand, she tapped the eraser against her chin. Aj looked over to her and smiled patiently.

"What's wrong Shorty?" asked Aj.

"I can't get this one," Leah replied as she stared lost at her paper. She looked into her sister's eyes and asked, "Can you help me with this last one?"

"Yes, let me see it."

Aj felt someone staring at her, so she looked up. The moment he captured her gaze, Ron smiled, a depraved smile, at her and walked away. Aj instinctively shivered in disgust before she continued helping her sister.

❧

The months passed and Aj kept herself busy as the spring holidays came and went. She painted eggs, enjoyed the cookouts, and especially loved the fireworks show her father put on at every event. She hung out with the twins, Layla and Paula at school, had sleepovers with Marie and Alexa every other weekend, worked after school, enjoyed her after school ceramics class, and played basketball.

Aj was on the winning team and her family was very supportive, as they showed up for almost every game. The playoffs came and went, at which Allen made sure to be in attendance. He proudly cheered his daughter on to victory. Aj brought home the winning trophy, after which, Allen, together with the other team member's parents, treated them to pizza. Aj could not have been happier that night.

❧

Aj passed from seventh grade to eighth before long, and she spent the summer working as many hours as the burger shop could legally allow. She bought her brothers and sister candy from the penny candy store and treated them to the movies where Marie often joined them. Aj and Marie hung out at the mall as often as they could. Alexa had landed a modeling contract, so they did not get to spend the night as often anymore. The twins spent the summer with their dad, however on the first day of school the girls began making up for lost time.

The fall holidays, family celebrations, wedding anniversaries, and football season was in full swing as Aj anxiously awaited her thirteenth birthday. She made it through each occasion by being as helpful to her mother as she could be and by occupying her time with anyone but Ron.

Aj enjoyed the company of her siblings and cousins, so much so, she and Marie took all who wanted to go out trick or treating. Everyone was dressed in their favorite costumes. She came home to Ron standing in the living room with his sunglasses on. Niyah ran to her dad and showed him her bag of candy. Marie and the other children sat on the living room floor and inspected their candy. Aj went to her room. As she walked past the kitchen she saw her mother, Coco, Lynn, and Nancy sitting at the table.

Aj continued to take note of Ron's comings and goings as to avoid an unaccompanied run in with him. She took heed of her Aunt Nancy's boisterous arrivals and listened for Ron's squeaky footsteps. No matter what the occasion or location, Aj doubled her efforts to avoid Ron like the plague. I am not going to let that man ruin my life, she affirmed.

☙

"Sweet thirteen," exclaimed Aj as she woke on the morning of her birthday. "I am officially a teenager, woo-hoo!"

Aj sprung out of bed and got ready for her day. Her mother made all of her favorites for breakfast, her father presented her with a gold birthstone jewelry set, and her brothers and sister made her a card. She was super excited all that day, and she felt loved. Her parents threw her a party at their house and everybody came. She could care less that Ron was there with his sunglasses on lurking. He looks like a nineteen eighty's reject with his jerry curl juice staining his collar, she thought after he entered the living room. She laughed to herself and turned her back to him.

Aj enjoyed her party, as she kept company with the family members she so loved and her school friends. Later that evening, they all piled into the cars and went to the roller-skating rink where her parents had purchased a birthday party package. The festivities continued on with cake and ice cream served at the rink. Aj skated with her brothers, sister, cousins, and friends. The DJ even shouted out her name. She could not have been more thrilled. As she lay her head down on the pillow that night, she thanked God and drifted off to sleep.

☙

Thanksgiving and Christmas were held at the Rashond's house that year, like most years and celebrations, the festivities went off without a hitch. The winter was cold that year and therefore Aj kept close to home, save for her job. She had become accustomed to Nancy and Ron showing up with their daughter unannounced and without cause, as they seemed to make her home their home away from home. Nancy did not cook, all she served were microwave meals, and therefore the Rashonds often hosted them for dinner.

One night, over dinner, Nancy made the announcement that she and Ron were expecting their second child. Everyone congratulated the couple with smiles all around, including AJ. Good, Aj immediately thought, maybe having another baby will keep you the hell away from me. After dinner, however, Aj still bribed one of her siblings to keep her company while she washed the dishes and rightly so. Just as she finished up, there Ron was at the entrance of the kitchen, staring at her.

"Come on Shorty," Aj said as she took her sister by the hand. "Let's go over your homework."

Leah leapt down from the chair and smiled up at her sister. When Aj looked up again, Ron was gone. The two girls spent the remainder of the evening in their bedroom. When they were done with Leah's assignments, they played checkers.

☙

Graduation day came and Aj was filled with excitement, as eighth grade graduation was a long-awaited milestone for her. She wore tan flowered capri pants, with a tan flower shirt, low wedge black heels, and applied her Smack big fat stick, lip gloss. Her hair was down in a wrap.

A week after her ceremony, where everyone who knew her seemed to be in attendance including both of her grandmothers, her parents threw a party at the YMCA, as the next week was her sister Leah's promotion ceremony from primary school to middle school. Aj happily shared the party with her sister. Aj was too delighted to care about Ron or his odd behavior. She focused on her sister and herself and the people who came to celebrate with them that evening.

☙

The Football preseason had long been awaited by the Rashond men. Allen, Christian, and Andre gathered in the basement in front of the big screen with snacks, soda and beer long before the game started. Every nuance about the football tournament, including the pre-game shows, was a must see. Even six-and-a-half-year-old Alani happily joined the guys in the man cave. Mabel whipped up hotdogs, sliders, nachos, or home baked pizza for her guys every game. One day Ron and Nancy showed up, unannounced, uninvited, and out of the blue. Mabel answered the door, and shortly thereafter Ron found his way to Aj's bedroom.

Almost two years had passed since Aj and Ron had been in the same room alone together, the moment only lasted for a few seconds before Marie ran back in from the kitchen with two cookies, one in each hand. However, in that time Ron set the stage. He pulled ten dollars out of his wallet, knelt, and handed it to Aj.

"What's this for," she asked rather curtly.

"I want us to be friends again," Ron said, to which Aj spied him suspiciously. "Just write me a thank you letter so I know we're still friends."

Ron smiled a sad smile, as if to convey regret. He acted like he wanted everything to go back to normal, but Aj did not trust him. She took the stance of, wait and see, only time would tell. Ron stood up and took a step back as Marie entered the room.

"Hi Uncle Ron," Marie greeted.

"What no spin today?" Ron replied.

Marie handed both cookies to Aj and went bounding and giggling into Ron's arms. He scooped her up and twirled her around. He placed her back on her feet, reached into his pocket and gave her two dollars, double what he normally gifted. As Aj sat on the bed looking on, she was lost in thought: Was he paying special attention to only me or did he treat Marie like that too? What about Siyah and Melanie?

No, Melanie is the same age as his daughter Niyah, she's just a little girl.

CHAPTER FOUR
WHY ME

As time passed Aj became more accepting of Ron always being around, after all he was family, married to her aunt, Nancy, and they seemed to be attached by the hip. The fact Ron and her father, Allen, had become friends, only added to the amount of time Ron spent at the Rashond's home. Ron always smiled his hello to Aj from a respectable distance. It was almost like he was the uncle that she loved again, although she forwent running into his arms for a hug and being swung around.

Aj could not get the night she and Marie played board games at her Aunt Nancy's house out of her head, no matter how much she tried. There was something about those moments in her life, the words Ron said to her and the manner in which he said them; and the inappropriate touches with his body pressed up against her, that simply did not feel right.

My aunt's husband is not supposed to put his hands on my waist and hug me from behind like that. I was never supposed to feel Ron's private parts pressed against my back. Nope, I don't trust him, Aj thought.

Every time Nancy and Ron visited the Rashond household, Ron asked Aj to write a thank you letter after he gave her five to ten dollars. As a kid, it meant a lot to have money to get chips and juice and go to the penny candy store, so Aj acquiesced to Ron's terms as a part of their familial relationship. All the while; after the first encounter alone with Ron at Nancy's house and being groped in her own parent's kitchen; she often wondered: Did Uncle Ron treat the other girls the same way he treats me? Did he ask any of the other girls in the family to wear certain clothes for him? Did Ron sneak up from behind and rub on them and stuff, or ask them to write thank you letters or was it just me?

Even though Aj never asked the other family members and they never knew what was going on with her, she felt compelled to protect her sister, Leah. Aj enjoyed being in The Troupe and she happily took her baby sister along with her when she was old enough to go. With Nancy and Ron visiting the Rashond's so often Aj did not want Leah left alone with him.

If he could say inappropriate things to me in his wife's home with her just down the hall, sneak around a cop's house, and find me alone so he can hug and touch on me, I can only imagine what he would say or do to my nine-year-old sister, she thought. I know Shorty will not be safe if Ron catches her alone. I must protect her.

Aj and Leah enjoyed The Troupes' program, as it kept them well occupied. The sister unity created an unbreakable bond, especially when they went out to sell cookies as a team, as it was the two of them competing against the troupe. As time passed, Aj focused on the fun of being together in the program with her sister, more than on protecting her. They took pride in their work, so much so, Leah joined Aj as one of the top ten salespeople her very first year.

☙

The evening of the annual Fourth of July family backyard barbeque was upon them. Every family member was in attendance. Allen worked the grill with Christian standing in as often as he was allowed. Mabel busied herself making sure everyone was well fed and happy. The younger children played with sparkles with Aj and Marie as supervisors. Nancy and Ron arrived late as usual.

"Hey y'all," Nancy bellowed out as sunglasses, tight t-shirt, and slacks clad, Ron, stood next to her holding their daughter. "We have an announcement," she continued which garnered everyone's attention. "It's a girl!" she finished as she cradled her stomach.

Everyone applauded, and one by one Nancy visited with her family member to get a personal congratulation. She basked in the spotlight; all the while Ron visited with the female children. He went from girl to girl, gave hugs and then spun them around, afterwards he gave out dollars. Aj was in the kitchen washing dishes as she looked out of the window in disgust, however moments later, she was bombarded by self-doubt.

She asked herself: Was I wrong? Did Uncle Ron just like my outfit that day? Was he just trying to steal a hug from time to time because I don't go to him anymore? Everybody seems to love him. They look so happy, like I was when I got swung around. But why did he say, "Don't tell no body?" I know my parents always say that what happens here in this house stays here in this house, so people are not gossiping about us or involving themselves in our family issues or throwing stuff in Mama and Daddy's face. I feel like there's something wrong with the way he acted, or he would not have told me not to tell. I need to talk to Aunt Coco about this.

Aj looked down to see that she was just about done washing the dishes. She smiled as she saw Marie outside waving at her. She put up her index finger signaling that she would be back outside in a moment. Marie returned the smile and offered two thumbs up before she turned away.

Ron's moment had come. While Aj finished up the pots and pans, Ron came around the corner to where she stood, with her back to the room. He walked up from behind her slowly, quietly, like a predator stalking its prey. He stood behind her for a long moment and inhaled the scent of her while she scrubbed baked on cheese out of a glass pan. He looked over his shoulder. The coast was clear. Ron stepped closer still, reached out and placed his hands on Aj's waist. Aj instantly froze. The dish slipped out of her hands and plopped under the water.

Her eyes grew wide as she thought: Oh my God what is going on? She looked down to see Ron's hands on her body. She tried to break free alas; she was trapped between her uncle and the sink. What do I do, Aj wondered frantically. She opened her mouth to scream and yet nothing came out. I'm trapped. Please someone help me, her mind and heart shouted. Help me Daddy! Someone please come back into this house.

Ron rubbed his hands over Aj's torso and breathed heavily against the back of her neck. As the seconds passed his presence, his actions, and his hot stinky breath made her stomach turned in disgust. Ron kissed the nape of Aj's neck. NO! No, no, no, no, her mind raced as her soul rejected everything about that moment. She squeezed her eyes shut and prayed Ron away: Lord please don't let this happen in my own house. Please don't let this man take me down. As Ron pressed his body against hers, Aj begged God even harder: Please God make Uncle Ron stop. He is not supposed to touch me like this. I am not his pregnant wife. Please get him off me Lord. Please don't let him do this to me with my mama and daddy standing right outside. Please God please, don't let Uncle Ron take my virginity from me! She prayed to the Heavenly Father for more than a minute before Ron finally released her. He wordlessly took a step back and looked down at her.

Aj turned around determined to face her attacker. I hate you, you are the devil, she pondered, her hands were balled into fists and anger reverberated from ever part of her being. Why would a grown ass man want to hug me like that? He shouldn't be coming on to a thirteen-year-old girl. She looked him in the eyes, but before she could utter a word, he pressed his finger to his lips.

"Remember, don't tell no body," Ron stated, with a depraved smile stretched across his face. He turned and walked out of the kitchen.

Aj stood there with her jaw dropped, staring after him for the longest moment, in total disbelief. She was left mentally shaken, emotionally damaged, and a little heart broken. She slowly turned around and finished washing the dishes, as she did not want to get yelled at for not having them done in a timely manner. Aj viscously scrubbed at the baked-on cheese lost in thought.

All of the people at this house and no one came walking this way… No one came to save me. My daddy is a police officer. He would have stopped Ron from putting his hands on me. No, he would have killed Ron and went to jail for murder. Mama doesn't have a job, so we would be homeless. They like locking up Black men, so I need to make sure I am never alone with Ron ever again. I have to keep it to myself, and don't tell no body, not even Marie and especially not my daddy. Why me? I feel like I'm being sexually bullied, but I don't understand why?

Aj batted back her tears as her mind raced. Oh God my feelings are so hurt right now. Why couldn't someone come in this kitchen and help me? Why couldn't I scream? I tried but nothing came out of my mouth. Aj stood there crying on the inside and fighting back her tears with her head bowed in shame.

Her mind flooded with thoughts. I've been keeping to myself, I bought my own bra, and I started wearing baggy clothes, so he wouldn't find me attractive. I wear my hair up in a ponytail. I hide my feet by wearing tennis shoes, anything just to cover up my body…

Did Ron just pick me because I'm quiet and shy? Ron was just so bold to put his hands on a cop's daughter. This just happened right under my daddy's nose and he has no idea what I'm going through, that a pedophile is sexually stalking me in my own home.

❧

While months passed without incident, Aj remained vigilant. She protected herself at all times, even when Ron was not present. Ron and Allen were buddies; Mabel and Nancy were sisters, and their children were Aj's first cousins. There was no way possible that she, as a teenage girl, could keep Ron away from her. No matter where she was, Nancy and Ron showed up.

In point of fact, one week while her parents vacationed for their wedding anniversary. Aj and her siblings stayed at Coco's house for the duration, as Coco was the go-to babysitter. Aj was glad to be in the company of her cousins and her favorite aunt. She loved playing outside and she even happily helped her aunt out around the house. Aj never minded washing the dishes and cleaning up behind the younger children, as it had become a routine part of her life.

At this aunt's house, she was able to be carefree, or so she thought. Coco cooked fried chicken, rice, corn bread, mac and cheese with red Kool Aid for a beverage. Aj was happy. She was in the kitchen washing dishes when lo and behold, Nancy and Ron happened by.

The moment Aj heard Nancy's predictable greeting, "Hey y'all!" she was frozen by panic, as for the first time in months, to her detriment, she had relaxed her diligence. She was in the kitchen alone. She knew that she was in danger and she felt trapped. Her instinct of fight or flight kicked in and she washed the dishes as fast as she could. All she wanted to do was to get out of that house, however, she knew that she could not leave her chores undone, as she did not want to disappoint her aunt.

"Hey Nancy, let me see my new niece," Coco greeted, as Nancy had just given birth to her daughter, Nia. "What brings you two by?"

"Girl, I need my hair done. This baby is wearing me out," Nancy said.

"How do you want it done?" Coco asked.

"I want it French braided to the back."

Coco styled everybody's hair in the family. Aj listened to Coco and Nancy talk, as she wiped down the counters and the kitchen table. She gathered the pots and pans off the stove and put them in the sink to soak while she washed down the stove and swept the floor. Nancy and Ron entered the kitchen with their children and sat them down at the table.

"Hi Aunt Nancy," Aj greeted, "hello baby Nia, hello Niyah," she continued as she helped get the baby settled into the highchair. "You want some mac and cheese?"

While Aj heated up some leftovers, Nancy returned to the kitchen with Ron in tow. Aj was relieved to have some company in the kitchen with her. She felt safe. Aj stood at the sink scrubbing caked-on grease out of the frying pan when she heard the squeak of Ron's footsteps approach. She scrubbed harder and faster as the squishy sound grew closer. It was the last unwashed item in the kitchen. Aj was almost home free when Ron walked up behind her. She could feel the heat of his body on her back. She could smell the stench of his cologne. She could feel his breath on her neck. Her stomach turned in repugnance. She closed her eyes and stilled herself.

God what can I do? If he touches me again I am going to scream, she thought as she readied herself for Ron's assault on her person. They stood there like that for the longest moment.

"When you go'n let me suck them titties," Ron whispered in Aj's ear.

Aj just froze, yet her mind raced: I can't believe what I just heard. "Huh?" she asked.

"When you go'n let me suck them titties," Ron asked again boldly.

Ron actually repeated what I thought he said, again, and to say that to me while his kids are sitting right here in this same room, at the kitchen table, right behind him, and his wife is in the living room a few feet away getting her hair braided, Aj pondered, makes him dangerous because he doesn't care. What kind of monster is my aunt married to? She felt her face turning red, and her heart pounded out of her chest. Aj gripped the handle of the pot but before she could muster the fortitude to turn and strike Ron, he was gone. Stricken with panic, Aj ran to the bathroom so no one would see her in such a state.

What has my life become, Aj wondered. It's like I am living in hell protecting myself against my aunt's husband who is trying to take me down. I have never felt so alone in my life. Why every time he sees me and I'm by myself Ron would come approach me not speak but put his hands on me?

At first, Ron would come over shoot pool, play darts with dad, act like he was going to the bathroom, and come upstairs to find me so he can get a kiss or rub on me or ask for a letter and now this? He stated his intentions very clearly. I must tell somebody. I cannot bear this alone. I'm just a little girl, an eighth grader. I am not a grown woman, and this is wrong. Everyone in my family always says, what happens in my house stays in my house. So, this happened to me in Aunt Coco's house and I'm going to tell her.

Later that evening Nancy and Ron were still at Coco's house. The children were in the living room with the adults, watching music videos. Coco was braiding Nancy's hair and Ron sat in a chair alone wearing sunglasses staring straight ahead.

Lil Bow Wow was the favorite rap artist at the time. Whenever his songs played all of the children got up and danced. Before long, it turned into a dance contest. Aj sat on the floor alone and watched on. She cheered her sister, Leah and although she wanted to join in she thought it best not to bring attention to herself, as she did not want to be a spectacle for Ron's entertainment.

Boom like an 808, by Blaq, began to play. Immediately, her sister and little cousins all begged Aj to dance with them, however she refused with a soft smile.

"What? Now, you too good to dance with your family," Nancy asked disparagingly.

"No ma'am," Aj replied, although she thought: I just don't want your creepy husband staring at me or touching me.

"Then get on up there Miss Prissy," Nancy ordered.

"Yes ma'am," Aj agreed. Her sad reluctance was lost on them all, everyone but Marie.

The children cheered and clapped. Everyone lined up to do the running man dance. Aj made sure to be as far off to the right as she could without actually leaving the room. She modestly crossed her arms over her breasts and danced along. Before long she danced and laughed along with her cousins.

When Aj looked up however, Ron's head was tilted in her direction. He was not watching the television. He stared hard and she could feel it. She felt dirty. Aj pretended to twist her ankle and returned to her seat on the floor. The moment she did she noticed that Ron's head turned toward the television once more.

In that moment Aj made up her mind: I have to talk to Aunt Coco tonight before bed. Nothing is going to stop me. I am going to tell!

Aj often worried about Leah and her other young female cousins. Is Ron staring at my little sister or my little cousin Siyah, she pondered.

Siyah was Coco's oldest daughter. She was ten years old with a lovely mocha complexion. She stood four feet and nine inches tall. Her hair was long and pretty.

And what about Melanie, Aj mused.

Melanie, Coco's youngest daughter, was mocha complexioned too with long Indian hair. Melanie used to go over to Nancy and Ron's apartment a lot because Nancy's daughter, Niyah, was the same age as Melanie. They had play dates and sleepovers.

Ron started doing this to me when I was just eleven years old and my little cousins are nine now, Aj thought. They are starting to grow into young ladies. How could Ron be attracted to young girls who are just starting puberty? Yes, I must tell. I just have to, Aj reaffirmed.

All I want to do is save all the little girls in my family from that nasty child molester. I know Aunt Coco will want to protect her daughters. She is a good mother and everyone's favorite aunt. She cares about us children.

At the end of the evening, once everyone had gone to bed, Aj went to Coco's room. She heard the television through the bedroom door. She knocked, poked her head in, and smiled.

"It's me Auntie," Aj timidly said.

"Whatever it is has to wait until tomorrow baby. I'm tired," Coco replied.

"Yes ma'am."

"We'll go shopping just the two of us, after I drop your cousins off at their grandmother's house."

Aj was happy with that and thus she smiled. She closed the door and went to bed. She did not fall asleep right away however, as she was lost in her thoughts: Did Ron see weakness in me that I am not bold and strong enough to take him on? Does he feel like I am the one he could escape with? And that I wouldn't tell no matter what he did to me? Aunt Coco won't let no man put his hands on me and get away with it.

Aj went to sleep reassured. The next morning Aj sat comfortably in the car with her Aunt Coco as they drove to the store. She played and replayed the events of the night before in her mind, and as she did her resolve strengthened. Aj was all set to turn the tides against Ron. Little did she know, soon thereafter, the backlash would be turned against her.

"Auntie, I have to tell you something," Aj began hesitantly.

"What is it Aj? You know you can tell me anything."

"The other day when Ron and Aunt Nancy came over, he came up behind me and said, 'When you go'n let me suck them titties?' and when I asked, 'Huh?' He boldly said it again."

Coco did not respond right away, as she could not quite believe the words she had just heard her niece utter. Instead she calmly pulled over the car Put it in park and looked into Aj's eyes. Her expression said, I know I didn't hear that right.

"What?" Coco asked.

"Last night when I was in the kitchen washing dishes, after Ron and Aunt Nancy came over, Ron came up from behind me and said, 'When you go'n let me suck them titties,' twice."

Coco put the car in drive, made a U-turn and zoomed back to the house. She jumped out of the car and rushed into the house. Not knowing what else to do, Aj followed suit. Am I in trouble, Aj wondered, her trepidation was clear in her stance. Coco called Ron.

"Hello," Ron answered.

"What the hell were you thinking talking to Aj like that?" Coco shouted, hostility radiated in her voice.

Ron stuttered badly as he said, "I was just kidding… I didn't mean it."

"This is a child, and you had no business speaking to her like that."

"I was just playing with her Coco."

"If you ever say something like that to Aj ever again I am going to get you."

Ron sputtered on and on about how he was not serious, and he was just joking however, he never offered an apology. Coco ended the call frustrated and angry. She turned to Aj, who was left standing there alone, and looked at her. Aj needed a hug and some reassurance that she was not in the wrong. All she wanted was to be comforted by her aunt, which is exactly what she did not get. What she received instead was something that she never saw coming. After all, what thirteen-year-old child would?

Coco simply mentioned, "I wish you would have said something earlier so that I could have said something to the both of them, Nancy and Ron together."

Aj did not respond. She just stood there respectfully as she thought: What grown man would play like that let alone say something like that to an eighth grader? He is definitely showing signs of a pedophile. Why can't you tell them together the next time you see them? Tell my parents! Tell everyone! Expose Ron for who he really is. Ron said, don't tell no body, but I stood up for myself. This happened to me in your house. Please help me!

ঌ

Once Aj's parents returned to town from their anniversary trip, the family celebrated July fourth at the Rashond house. Everyone was in attendance including Nancy and Ron. Aj tried her level best to ignore Ron. She continued to avoid him like the plague. Her eyes helplessly cut in his direction as hate filled her heart. I have to see this man again after what he just said to me that day? How can my parents invite that man back into our home after what he did? Aj turned to leave the room however she was halted by her mother.

"Aj?" Mabel called out.

"Yes ma'am?"

"Coco told me what happened between you and your Uncle Ron." Aj's heart filled with hope. Finally, someone is coming to my rescue she thought. Aj felt as if a knife was being sunk into her back as she listened to her mother's next words, "Someone said that you said Ron kissed you on the cheek and you are upset now."

Mabel scolded Aj for not wanting to be touched. Somehow Aj's words got twisted up after she told Coco the truth. Coco conveyed a completely different story to her sister, Aj's mother. In an effort to protect her sister, Nancy, Coco painted a whole different picture of the situation, one which was entirely the opposite of what truthfully happened because she did not want the truth to come out and ruin Nancy's marriage. Coco rationalized that she had handled the situation and therefore Nancy did not have to get hurt.

"Why didn't you tell me first?" asked Nancy saddened.

"You need to apologize for hurting Nancy's feelings," Mabel insisted.

Why do I have to say sorry for something he did, Aj thought although she obeyed reluctantly, "I'm sorry Aunt Nancy."

Aj's whole being simultaneously filled with hurt, anger, and disbelief as she stood there vilified by the very people who were supposed to protect her. How can this be, she asked herself. How is it that I ended up apologizing to Aunt Nancy and saying I'm sorry, but I didn't do nothing wrong? Damn this family is crazy and weird.

CHAPTER FIVE
WHO DID YOU TELL

Aj found no solace in her home, as she no longer trusted her family; after all, they were the very people who chose to protect a pedophilic predator. She often told friends about the situation she found herself in with Ron. The years of pedophilic stalking, Ron boldly ingratiated himself into her life by pretending to be friends with her father—a friendship which started immediately after the one and only time Aj spent the night under her Aunt Nancy and Uncle Ron's roof and ended shortly after Aj told her Aunt Coco the ugly truth.

Three years of sexual bullying: the inappropriate touches, kisses on the neck, hugs from behind, the stares from behind his dark glasses. Aj resented the fact that Ron's hands had been on her body. Antipathy welled up in her heart every time she remembered those words, "When you go'n let me suck them titties?"

No matter how hard Aj tried, she could not suppress the memory of the perverted degenerate who all but ruined her relationships over the years. She could not confide in her parents, or siblings. She just knew that her friends would never understand or see her in the same way ever again. No one wants to be viewed as damaged.

It was easier for her to tell strangers because they did not know her family. Strangers did not judge nor did they shift the blame on the adolescent victim.

Thankfully, Ron never touched her again; however, Aj was left to endure his presence at every family function. She felt as if living with years of sexual abuse and sharing her story with strangers was not good enough. Aj needed to escape to be heard.

Mabel's brother Daniel, the family called him Buddy, hosted the family Christmas dinner at his house that year. He presented Aj with a custom sized dollhouse and assembled it before everyone arrived.

"This is for you Aj," Daniel smiled as he spoke. "I wanted you to see how it looks all put together."

"Thank you, Uncle Buddy," Aj replied as she threw her arms around her uncle and hugged him tight. "I love it."

The dollhouse was fully furnished with three levels. As the night passed Aj happily played with her gifts. She was lost in just being a child when the next thing she knew the doorbell rang.

"Hey y'all," Nancy bellowed.

Resentment filled Aj's heart as she closed her eyes and quietly said goodbye to her happy Christmas. She had long since grown to begrudge the sound of her aunt's voice as she never appeared at any occasion without Ron. Aj looked up and saw Ron and Nancy with their two daughters coming through the door. Aj was on full alert. She watched as she recalled a sermon in church. Watch therefore, you do not know when the master of the house is coming, in the evening, at midnight, at the crowing of the rooster, or in the morning; lest, coming suddenly, he finds you sleeping. And what I say to you, I say to all: Watch! Watch, stand fast in the faith, be brave, be strong. Ron was not Aj's master, he was her tormentor. She promised herself to be brave and strong like the bible said and to never let Ron catch her slipping.

The first thing Ron did was make a plate to eat. Daniel provided a nice spread for their Christmas meal. He made mac and cheese, yams, greens, and a menagerie of soul food. Nancy never cooked; she always made tv dinners because she couldn't cook at all. Ron had prepared four plates and proceeded to the living room. He called Aj in there and gave her five dollars.

What is this, Aj wondered, hush money, guilt? Aj took the money once Nancy was in full view. She looked at her aunt, her gaze all but shouted, you see him, right?

"Why you give her that and not give her brothers and sister no money?" Nancy asked.

Aj turned and saw Ron reach in his pocket to give her sibling money as well. She smiled as she thought: Ron had no intention of giving them money, but Aunt Nancy made him do it. He never had a say so on nothing whatsoever. Like a dog, come, sit, heal, give your money. You will never get me alone ever again, you troll. What kind of woman would even want a man like you?

Aj was fourteen years old and she had grown into her own. After Christmas, Ron appeared to no longer have interest in her. She had gotten too confident for him to take advantage of. As time passed Ron seemed scared of Aj's boldness and assertion. He liked quiet, shy, and innocent little girls who were too scared to tell. Although Aj worried about her sister and younger cousins, life went on.

Aj slowly approached high school. The holidays were over, the basketball season ended with a championship trophy, and she had finally found peace in her home. She worked at a different fast food restaurant, continued her sports, became a wiz at ceramics and maintained her friendships as her transference ritual from eighth grade to high school came to pass.

Aj was alone as a freshman, as her favorite cousin, Marie, would not follow until the next year and her grade school friends attended different high schools.

Aj was fresh meat, and as tradition would have it, all the seniors tried to scare the new incomers who did not have any family members or friends in attendance. Eventually, Aj made a few friends that rode the school bus with her. She met a girl named Dee who was a sophomore and became good friends. Dee lived around the corner from Aj and yet they never met before then. She met a girl named Shana and they became best friends. They went shopping together, hung out at the mall, and talked on the phone. Neither one of them drove just yet, and therefore had no choice but to catch the city bus. Aj did not mind, as long as she was free.

Even with all of the time she spent, and all of the conversations with Dee, Aj never brought up her experiences with Ron. She was happy to remove the situations from her mind and simply enjoy being a teenager doing teenage things. Aj and Dee were like two peas in a pod as they enjoyed high school and everything teenage life encompassed.

By and by, during her sophomore year in high school, another rite of passage presented itself in Aj's life, she met a boy. JP was tall and skinny with long hair. He was street smart, book smart, and enjoyed sports. JP would often take Aj to the Buck's basketball games. One evening he decided to go watch her play basketball, as he wanted to see what her hooping skills were like, so he accompanied her to a game.

"You look like you sit on the sidelines and cheer," JP teased.

"Ok we'll see," Aj replied with a knowing smile.

JP watched on impressed by Aj's dexterity. Once the game had come to an end, he went to her. He smiled all the way.

"Wow, I didn't know you can play so well, but you're still not better than me," he challenged.

Aj smiled happily. JP tried to give her a kiss however she stepped back. She frowned at him disapprovingly.

"What's wrong? Do I got something on my lips or something?"

"I don't like kissing," Aj replied despondently.

"Why?"

Aj was hesitant to tell JP. She considered what he might do to Ron, as if Ron didn't deserve what was coming his way. She mustered up her courage and looked into JP's eyes.

"Ron used to kiss and rub on me inappropriately," Aj stated boldly.

"Who is Ron?" he asked.

"My uncle," she answered flatly.

"I'm going to drive over there and beat his ass." JP was rowdy and ready.

"No, don't."

"Are you sure?"

"Yes, just leave it alone. I don't want you going to jail over that low life."

The ride home was unbelievably quiet. JP had a mad expression plastered on his face. He really wanted to hurt someone, and Aj could feel the energy beaming off him. They arrive at her house and she leaned over and gave him a kiss on the cheek. She wanted him to feel at ease. Aj needed the night to end on a good note, as Ron had ruined so many moments in her life. She refused to allow him to tarnish her time with JP.

☙

One day, a little over two years after Coco had confronted Ron and then swiftly swept his pedophilic behavior under the rug, Aj and Leah were babysitting their cousin, Melanie. Melanie was having a bath, when all of a sudden, Aj and Leah heard this loud cry coming from the bathroom. Leah went to investigate and called Aj in there.

"She just started crying out of nowhere," Leah said. "I don't know what's wrong."

Aj asked gently, "Melanie what's wrong? Why were you crying?"

Melanie tried to talk but could not because the tears would not stop flowing.

"Calm down Melanie." Aj cooed. "What happened?"

"When I was at Aunt Nancy's house taking a bath…" she whimpered, "and when I got out the tub Ron… Ron…" Melanie voice trailed off. She sobbed woefully and did not say anything else. Melanie was petrified, panicky, and shaking. "Please, please don't tell my mom," she begged.

Ron had moved on to easier prey like a thief in the night. Melanie was a shy girl, sweet and loving.

She liked to play with dolls and her cousin Niyah. Sleepovers at Aunt Nancy and Uncle Ron's house were a regular occurrence, as they were as close as sisters. Ron found his perfect victim, a child who would not tell.

Aj's recollection of Ron's depraved behavior and the aftermath flashed into her mind as if it had only happened yesterday. In that moment, his words, "Remember, don't tell," rang in her ears as if he was standing right behind her. She recalled how the story was changed to appease Nancy. She thought about Coco's initial response, the anger, the threat that may have saved her. All she wanted to do was protect her cousin from the shame of it all without humiliating her.

Aj and Leah believed that they could not tell Coco because they knew Coco would have acted a fool, cussed Ron out, and made a lot of loud threats, but ultimately, Coco would have told everyone in the family and shamed Melanie or just swept it under the rug. Coco would not have done anything to get justice for her daughter, after all she too was raised by a child molester. She and her sisters were raised to turn their backs on the truth and groomed not to tell.

Aj also knew how Coco had handled the situation when it was her turn. There was no comfort, no sympathy, just blame the victim. What did you do to make that man come into that bathroom with you? Why didn't you lock the door? Aj wanted to spare her cousin those questions. She wanted to save her cousin from being blamed for not protecting herself. Melanie was so quiet and shy that Aj knew Melanie could not bear her mother's anger and therefore Aj and Leah chose not to tell Coco what Melanie told them. They kept Melanie's secret and stayed quiet about that day even amongst themselves.

☙

Unfortunately, that night was the beginning of the end for Aj and JP. After witnessing the trauma Melanie experienced, Aj was not inclined towards male affections. She was forever tainted by the sexual delinquencies of the man she had once loved and admired, her uncle. Her aunt's husband, a man who had been a part of her family since before she was born had affectively changed how she viewed and interacted with the male species evermore.

As the relationship between Aj and JP should have progressed, it staggered, faltered and died. There were no jealousies between them, there was however the absence of warmth. JP wanted to show his care and admiration to his girlfriend, however every time he made an attempt to hug or kiss her, he was affronted by her rejection. Although he tried to be understanding, loving even, in the end he gave up on her. He saw her as damaged beyond what his teenage mind could repair or even comprehend.

The missed lunches, unmade calls, and rescheduled dates which never seemed to manifest all took their tolls. Little by little Aj and JP disappeared from each other's lives. There was no one to blame between the two, as life went on they respectively chose to move one without one another. The mutual, gradual ghosting of each other was easier for Aj and JP than goodbye. She helplessly watched as the first boy that she ever liked slipped away, out of her life. Aj often wondered how one loses contact with a person who goes to the same school.

Junior year was upon Aj and she was very excited to finally be an upper classman. She focused on school, sports and her employment. She wanted a better life than the one that was provided for her. She had goals, dreams, ambitions, and of course a social life. Aj was busier than ever. She traveled mostly by city bus, as she did not want to ask anyone for anything unless it was absolutely positively necessary. Aj made her own money, she had reliable transportation, and she preferred the company of friends and strangers over family.

Aj was on the city bus, on her way to school, one day during her junior year. The bus was super packed, there were no more open seats left. Out of the blue, a boy pulled her over to him.

"You can sit on my lap," he said with a smile. "My name is Giorgio."

"Hi, I'm Aj," she said as she smiled and took a seat.

Giorgio was big and tall, light skinned, stood six feet and three inches tall, and weighed about two hundred ninety pounds. He looked mean, until he smiled at her. Giorgio made Aj feel protected. He called her on the house phone later that evening. They spoke for hours about teenage things. Aj was happy that they met.

"It's time for me to get to bed," Aj said.

"Before you go I want to ask you, will you be my girlfriend?"

"Yes," Aj replied happily.

"Bet. I'll take you to the movies this weekend."

"Okay, see you in the morning before class, goodnight."

"Goodnight."

Aj's relationship with Giorgio started off well. He took her to the movies, and he bought her just because gifts. He was just the guy everyone liked and got along with, although he did not play sports.

One day before their junior year came to an end, Giorgio went up to Aj while she stood at her locker. He hugged and kissed her from behind, which immediately reminded her of the torment she suffered through during her adolescence. Aj pushed the thoughts out of her mind, turned around and smiled.

"I miss you so much Aj," Giorgio said.

"I miss you too," Aj said as she gave him a hug.

"Would you like to go to prom with me?" he asked.

"Yes!" Aj replied happily.

She gave him a big hug and a kiss on the cheek. *I know people have often mistaken Giorgio for bully because he is so big but, in the inside, he is nice and sweet,* Aj mused. *I can't believe I am going to prom with the most popular dude in school!*

Aj wore an orange dress and Giorgio wore a white suit with an orange tie. He picked her up in a red Camaro. He brought her a corsage which matched her dress. They had the best time, one of their last moments together, as Aj received an opportunity to transfer schools her senior year, so she could graduate early. She loved the fact that her school day was only four hours long, because it gave her time to work a full-time job.

❧

High school graduation was upon Aj. It was time to leave high school and start her college journey. She applied to St. Paul College in Minnesota and not only got accepted, she was awarded a scholarship. Sadly, because one of her cousins did not want to go, Aj turned down the opportunity to attend.

Undaunted, Aj applied to Sanford Brown College, she wanted to enroll in their Criminal justice program. Once she was accepted she happily told her family. Regrettably, her own aunt, Coco, advised her against attending.

"You should not waste your time doing that. You'll be in school forever," Coco said.

"It is a good program that will give me a good future," Aj responded.

"It is too much work, you will be in college for years."

"I thought a good education was well worth it."

"At Kaplan college you can be a medical assistant and it is only a nine-month program."

While attending Kaplan, Aj worked at a halfway house for women in transition from prison. It was mandatory that the ladies complete a ninety-day program before their release back into society. The facility provided many aids to help with the adaptation to modern civilization: social interaction, transportation aid, employment assistance, and psychological counseling.

The facility provided on sight counselors who were available several hours per day, five days per week. There was an open-door policy, no pressure, no obligation. Aj wanted to talk to someone about her issues. She wanted to unburden herself of the pain and anguish she had faced and lived with for the past ten years. Aj found herself staring in the general direction of the counselor's offices as the memories of what Ron used to do and say to her coursed through her mind. After all of the years that had passed the pain was still fresh, the betrayal still bothered her.

"What's wrong," a woman asked, her voice was kind and filled with concern.

Aj looked into the woman's gentle accepting face and categorically broke down crying. Her head dropped, her shoulders slumped, and her arms dangled at her sides lifelessly as she cried. The counselor wrapped an arm around Aj's shoulder and escorted her to a private space.

Every repugnance Aj had faced in her short life flooded out, raw and unfiltered. She detailed the intimate horrors of her childhood from the first sadistic transgression that happened with in her aunt's house while her aunt was in the next room, down to the last betrayal in front of her family when she was forced to apologize to a child molester and his wife. Aj took a deep breath and squeezed out her remaining tears. She batted her eyes clear as she attempted to focus. She took the tissues from the counselor, sat down, and dried her face. Aj looked up and smiled a genuine smile for the first time in years.

"Wow, I feel better. Thank you," Aj confessed.

"I'm glad," the counselor stated sincerely.

"How did you know?"

"There is a prevalence of childhood sexual abuse among incarcerated females in the prison system. There's a look… and you had that same look on your face."

"Oh," Aj sighed. "What do I do now? How do I get that victimized look off my face?"

"You have already taken the first step."

"I want everyone to know. I need my parents to know what happened to me."

"If you were to tell the family now, it would do you more harm than good."

"Harm? But what about me," asked Aj, outraged. "Don't I matter? Why should I spare his family and his feelings? They need to know! Why do he get to walk around free and sleep great at night? I used to wake up in the middle of the night punching the wall because I would have bad dreams that I was punching Ron in the face and when I woke up I had bruised knuckles. Eventually, I just didn't say nothing at all, but I wanted to so bad! I told you that I went to someone I trusted in my family and told them, but they just swept it underneath the rug because they didn't want to make Nancy mad or break up her marriage and now you tell me to keep my mouth shut too?" Indignant, Aj stood to her feet, looked into the counselor's eyes, and hissed, "*He* said don't tell!"

༺

Years passed and Aj pressed on with her life sharing parts of her story with select elder family members and mostly strangers, in an attempt to divest the hurt and pain that she carried every day of her life. In that time, she met a man, Wayne, and their friendship blossomed. One night over dinner he announced that he was moving to Arizona. He asked her to go with him. Aj did not give an immediate response as she needed to think it over and talk to her family.

Aj lay in her bed lost in thought. I am going to move to Arizona. I am tired of the snow and tired of being cold. I am twenty-five years old and this is my opportunity to go out there and see. I have been talking to Wayne for about six years now and he is a good man. I can trust him. He will make sure I'm okay. It really is time for me to go. I am so tired of my family not believing me, thinking that I would make up Ron's sexual aggressions against me, when I was an adolescent girl. If only Melanie and Niyah would tell their truths…

As luck would have it Aj's friend from high school, Nadea, lived in Phoenix. She was married, and they had a huge dog, a golden retriever. Aj was secretly happy not to be truly alone and dependent on a man, as before long Wayne's company did not do so well and he ended up moving back to Milwaukee to the original clientele. Although Aj was gainfully employed and acclimated well to her new life, Wayne asked if she wanted to move back home with him. She kindly declined his offer. Aj decided to stay in Phoenix and figure it out. While Aj searched for an apartment, she stayed with her friend and her husband for a couple of months.

One evening Aj, Nadea and her husband were sitting at home. They had made it through the work week and had no plans for the weekend. The mister was settled in as he was a homebody.

"Let's get up and go out," Nadea said out of the blue.

Aj really was not feeling it, but she got up, hit the shower, and got dressed, as did Nadea. Her husband dropped them off at the club. They were there for a good couple of hours and had a couple of drinks, after which Nadea called her husband to come and get them. They lived almost 40 minutes away from the club. On the ride home, everyone was tired as ever. Aj sat in the back seat drifting off to sleep.

The next thing Aj knew, she heard this big boom. Someone ran their car into theirs from behind. Their car hit the highway median and flipped over. The car that rear ended them kept going, a hit and run. Two cars pulled over and stopped to help. With assistance, one by one the three made it out. Aj had a panic attack.

I can't believe I was just in a rollover car accident, she thought. I have to catch my breath. Aj looked at her surroundings and the people gathered around as she continued processing what had just happened. Wow I'm able to walk away from this car accident. I knew God wasn't finished with me. I'm here for a purpose. I have a story to tell. My time is not up!

The three were transported to the nearest hospital by ambulance. Unfortunately, the ambulance which carried Aj shut off completely while driving, at least twice. Are they serious, Aj asked herself, what kind of ghetto ambulance is this? Must be a trap one, Aj surmised as she tryed to find humor in the situation. Aj laughed to keep from crying.

Once she finally made it to the hospital, they rushed her into the trauma room, checked for any broken bones, fractures, and concussions. Gladly, Aj only suffered bumps and bruises. Her body was sore as heck. It took a while for her to recover and get back to her normal self mentally and physically. Once her parents found out that she was in a car accident, they flew her up to Milwaukee to make sure she was alright.

CHAPTER SIX BREAKING POINT

Four years had passed since Aj moved to Arizona. In her heart of hearts, she knew that Milwaukee had never truly been an option. She loved her life in the Phoenician desert town of Mesa, as she had met and made some great friends. Alas, she did not have any family locally, no one close to call her own. Her life lacked personal closeness—intimacy. Before long a sort of loneliness set in.

It was a big move for one person to start their life by themselves in a new city thousands of miles away from home, Aj mused, but I did it. I am here all alone. She looked around her well furnished apartment and smiled. I'm ready for a relationship. Maybe even start a family of my own. I'm twenty-eight years old and single with no kids. My biological clock is ticking… Yes, I'm ready to start my family. I desire to be a mother but how am I going to meet mister right?

Aj decided to try a dating app for fish in the sea. She uploaded a few pictures and before long the first guy commented on her profile. Certain men on the dating app really wanted to have a serious relationship. On the other hand, there were some guys who just wanted to have sex. They were very brazen about their sexual desires, which Aj thought was really disgusting. Aj went on two dates.

Aj met her first date, Darrius, at the casino. He was a twenty-eight-year-old barber from Atlanta who stood five feet five inches tall. They spent the evening enjoying the excitement and ambiance of the Native American Gaming establishment. They gambled, took in a show, and enjoyed a nice dinner. Aj won a couple of hundred dollars playing the slots. The comedy show left them in hysterics, after which, her date offered to treat her to dinner. Over dinner they talked, laughed, and got better acquainted.

It is nice being with someone my own age, Aj thought as she smiled into Darrius' eyes. I am looking forward to getting to know him better. I can definitely see myself going on a second date with him.

She excused herself to the bathroom. He waited for her at the bar. Upon her return he stood up and tried to go in for a kiss, which she easily dodged. He reluctantly settled for a hug.

"I ordered you a glass of wine," Darrius said.

"I hope you're not trying to get me drunk," Aj replied sweetly.

In that moment the bartender placed two glasses of wine on the bar before them. Darrius smiled sheepishly as he slid a glass closer to Aj. She eyes the wine suspiciously.

"Just one glass won't hurt after the dinner we just had," Darrius begged.

"Okay, just one glass." Aj took a sip and smiled as she leaned in closer. "Tell me more about your life here in Arizona. Why are you still single?"

Their conversation went on for another hour and the date went well until the very end when Aj learned that Darrius had six children by four different women. She was utterly turned off and ready to leave. How can you be out here paying for a lavish date when you've got mouths to feed, she wondered?

"It's getting late…" Aj began.

"I got a room for us," Darrius stated as he held Aj close.

"What do you mean us?" she asked, put off.

"You can't tell me you ain't feeling me."

"I think you're nice and all but…"

"But what," he began hostilely, "all of a sudden you're not feeling me?" He pulled her close and tried to kiss her however she resisted with a frown. "You know what this is."

"This isn't that, so I'm leaving," Aj replied and yanked free of his hold. "Good night, and no there will be no second date so lose my number."

There are way too many perverts in this world. A hotel room on the first date, really? I know there are good men out there. I deserve better than you Darrius. I am not broken, I am not desperate, and I'm damn sure not ugly; Aj thought on the drive home.

The very next day, Aj popped back on the dating app and accepted a date with another man. The second date was at a park. Aj and Morgan walked around, talked, and worked out. Morgan was a warehouse worker who stood six feet and two inches tall. He had silky smooth dark skin and a beautiful smile. He really is an interesting fella, Aj thought after their conversations, however, he just wasn't it. There's no spark. I'm going to log back on the dating app and check some more messages.

Aj had about ninety messages, most of them trite. While she scrolled, she clicked delete until she came across a couple of interesting messages.

Leon: Good morning queen, how is your day going so far?

I'm a little puzzled. He called me Queen, she thought happily, I am going to reply.

Aj: Good morning to you too.

Aj and Leon exchanged phone numbers. They spoke on the phone often. In that time Aj learned that Leon was a chef. As their interests grew in one another they called more.

"What part of the valley you staying in," asked Leon.

"Mesa," Aj replied.

"Wow, I live in Mesa too."

"What's your cross streets?"

As it turned out they lived only five minutes away from each other. Leon invited Aj over, though she was very skeptical, as she usually met people in public places. Their conversation continued and Aj thought, I didn't get that criminal vibe from him, so I will go see him. Aj and Leon talked for about two hours outside at the park by his apartment complex. It was getting late and they both had to go to work the next day. He walked her to her 2015 SUV.

"Oh, nice whip," Leon complemented.

"Thank you, I just got it."

"I hope to see you again."

"I hope to see you again too."

Aj smiled all the way home. Eventually, Aj and Leon went on more dates. They went to the movies and out to dinner. There were times when he would invite her over to his place after she got all dressed up, as she thought they were going somewhere, only to watch the internet TV. What a waste of an outfit, Aj thought, although she was happy to be in his company.

Aj had a trip voucher that she had not yet used, although she meant to. The voucher was for round trip travel to any of the surrounding cities. She decided to go to San Diego because it was only five hours away and she did not have to spend money on flights. One day, as Aj and Leon spent more and more time together, she worked up the courage to broach the subject of taking their first trip together as a couple.

"Would you like to go on a trip with me?" Aj asked.

"Sure," Leon agreed right away, "when?"

"This weekend, we could leave Friday when I get off work."

As Friday approached Aj mind raced: There's a lot of stuff I must get done to my car like an oil change, and tire rotation. I want this to be a smooth trip without being stranded on the side of the road with the tire blown out. She was even more excited on the day of.

So yeah, Friday is here and I'm super excited about my trip and I get to leave early too on a Friday. Now that I'm a medical assistant at a neurology clinic it is very hard to leave early on a Friday, but I worked it out. I have checked the voicemail messages and returned the patient and client calls. I asked the other medical assistants to cover for me and for the first time, I am leaving with peace of mind.

Leon was outside waiting for Aj when she came out. They did not get straight on the road because she wanted to go home, shower, get out of her scrubs, and put on comfortable traveling clothes. After they arrived at her apartment, Aj realized she had forgotten to pack. While they were only going to be gone a day and a half, Aj packed five outfits.

"You need those many clothes?" Leon asked.

"You never know who you might see or where you might go," Aj said and laughed out loud. "Yes, I do."

As Aj and Leon headed down the three flights of stairs, laden down with suitcases, to the parking lot Aj thought: For some reason I wanted to live on the third floor, but I did it for the exercise. I will never live in an apartment on the third floor ever again. This sucks... It sucks when you got a lot of groceries and bags to carry. Next time…

Once the car was all gassed up Aj and Leon hit the highway. It was about five p.m., and therefore they estimated that they would arrive in San Diego at about ten p.m.

"We have five hours to talk and get to know one another more, about any and everything," Aj began.

"Okay. Do you want kids and if so how many?" Leon asked.

"I want four or five children. I want a real big family because I come from a real big family and kids need playmates," she said, after which she thought: It's so sudden to be even talking about kids isn't it? But this is just talk. After all, Leon is only twenty-seven years of age. I expect this conversation from older guys.

Although Aj tried to remain excited about their trip and engage in conversation, she fell quiet and soon after Leon fell asleep. Aj was left with her thoughts. Unfortunately for her, Uncle Ron's treachery haunter her mind, body, and soul still. She often thought about the effects of his predatory pedophilic advances had on her everyday life and potential love.

Maybe because Ron touched me inappropriately at a very young age, I have found myself attracted to guys about thirty and over. I don't know if I am looking for understanding now that I am old enough to know what his true intentions were or normalcy, a normal relationship with a man that age. When I was nineteen and was talking to someone twenty-seven, my family just thought the twenty-seven-year-old was just way too old for me. Any and every one had something to say accusing him of being a pedophile for dating a nineteen-year-old. They said he needed to find someone his own age but where was that care and concern when I was a ten-year-old little girl and Ron was in his thirties, but he sexually stalked me for three years. Now that's a pedophile. Any who, I think I finally found the one, someone that will be a great husband and a great father.

Now I hate driving for long periods of time, I'd rather fly and get there quicker in about three hours or less because driving is so boring, but we have finally made it! Let me wake this man up so we can get checked in. I am going to enjoy being with this lovely man for the weekend and try my best to build something real with him.

Aj and Leon could not do much in the way of dining and entertainment because it was too late, and a lot of places were closed. They called it a night. The next morning came and Leon was a wake up bright and early kind of person. He woke at six forty-five in the morning.

All I want to do is sleep, Aj thought, but this is a getaway, so I really can't. Let me get up, get dressed, and head to the beach to put my feet in the sand.

Moments later they were standing on the beach looking out over the horizon. Just look at the ocean, it's just so beautiful, just breathtaking, Aj thought. I actually wouldn't mind living out here, but it is expensive.

Aj and Leon ran along the beach and swam in the water. Hours seemed to pass like minutes as they thoroughly enjoyed one another's company. Somehow two of her fingernails got broken on their excursion. She had not noticed until they were leaving the beach.

"I want to stop and get my nails done. I have two broke down that need to be fixed and I can't go around out of town looking ratchet," Aj said as they made their way to the highway.

We don't have time for that," Leon replied displeased.

"Yes, we do. We'll make time."

It only took the nail tech twenty minutes to repair two nails. Aj walked over to Leon and saw that he was so agitated. She could not do anything but laugh.

"Let's go check out the mall," she suggested.

"Okay," he said with a smile.

They went into a couple of stores and tried on a few outfits. The joy quickly returned to their outing. Aj exited the dressing room in a lovely orange sundress and struck a pose. Leon looked at her approvingly.

"One thing about living in Arizona is that you don't have to buy too many jeans and long sleeve shirts because it's just so hot. Literally, you can wear a summer dress every day without checking the weather," Aj commented.

"You should definitely get that one!" Leon said.

Their first trip to California came to an end. Although they wanted to continue exploring it was time to head back to Arizona, because they both had work on Monday morning.

I hate getting in so late just to get up at six thirty in the morning. I can't believe it is already midnight. I had fun though, it was worth it. Leon is a good man. This trip was my best idea yet.

A year had passed. Aj's and Leon's relationship had flourished, in fact she was pregnant with her first child. Although she had been raised to believe that people must be with someone for years in order to get married or have a child, she could not be happier. She called her mom and dad and waited for them both to get on the line so that she could tell them at the same time.

"I have some good news, I'm pregnant," Aj stated happily.

"Congratulations baby girl," Allen said.

"When are you due?" asked Mabel.

"My expected due date is on October 17th."

"When are you coming back here?" asked Allen.

"Yes, when are you coming home?" echoed Mabel.

They were excited as this child would be both Allen's and Mabel's first grandchild. The happy response from her parents spurred Aj on. She called her sister Leah and then her best friend Shana. Aj and

Shana had been best friends since freshman year in high school and they told each other everything.

"I want to plan the baby shower here in Milwaukee," Shana said, excited.

"Are you serious?" Aj asked, surprised.

"Yes, think about it. Most of your family lives here in Milwaukee. Come on, let me do this for you."

"Okay Shana, you're on," Aj agreed wholeheartedly. "So, the baby shower is going to be there in Milwaukee."

Aj and Shana were on the phone for two hours. The talked about the baby shower, and made all sorts of plans: location, theme, and guest list.

"Who is not invited?" Shana asked.

"I don't want Ron to come or your brother's girlfriend. You know I really can't stand her. But Ron is not allowed no matter what," Aj stated emphatically. She continued on with conviction, "He does not get to celebrate my happiness with me. I'm bringing a beautiful baby into this world and I don't want to continue to carry the burden of having to see him again while I'm pregnant. Aunt Nancy is still invited, but her husband cannot come."

"Okay Aj, as you wish, no Ron no matter what."

"Thank you, Shana, this is a new start for me."

After Aj got off the phone with Shana, she immediately called Shana's mom, Darla. Aj shared the news of her pregnancy and informed her that Shana had graciously offered to host the baby shower there in Milwaukee. Once the congratulations and euphoria died down the conversation became very serious.

"Miss Darla, Ron is not allowed to come to the baby shower."

She asked, "Why?"

Aj told Darla what her loving uncle used to do to her when she was a child. She gave every gory detail of how she was sexually stalked, inappropriately touched, and kissed on the neck every time she was caught alone, and how after she told her truth, the particulars of her three-year ordeal were twisted, distorted into misunderstood niceties, and then turned against her.

"How come you didn't say anything sooner?" asked Darla.

"I didn't tell because I was so scared," Aj said batting back the tears that welled up in her eyes almost instantly. "Ron always told me not to say anything, but I did anyway. So, my own family turned against me… and I didn't want to keep reliving it over and over again."

"What about your mother?"

"I'm expecting my mom to tell Aunt Nancy why her husband can't come."

As time passed the pregnancy progressed nicely, save for the fact that Aj threw up all day and night. Every time she opened up the refrigerator she had to vomit. The first trimester came and went quite quickly.

This baby is really kicking my butt, Aj thought. Being nauseated and constipated is no joke. Not being able to poop, this must be a girl the way I'm feeling. I want to find out what I'm having so I can start buying stuff for my baby's room. I've been searching online for a place that will let me find out what I'm having at 15 weeks. I've got to find out as soon as possible.

Aj ended up calling this place called Blue's Clues. She scheduled an appointment for an ultrasound. She called her boyfriend, Leon, and let him know that they had an appointment scheduled soon.

"So, we get to find out if the baby is a boy or a girl right then and there?" Leon asked, super excited.

"Yes," Aj replied with a little giggle of joy.

Aj and Leon arrived at Blue's Clues, their hearts filled with anticipation. The tech entered the lobby and walked over to them. She escorted them to the ultrasound room.

"What do you think it is?" the tech asked.

"A girl, because I'm way too sickly," Aj replied.

"Let's take a look and see." The tech put the ultrasound on Aj's stomach and rolled it around. "She's being wild, still acting up I see," she continued as she looked at the monitor and moved the wand this way and that. "Just jumping and moving around and.... There! It is a boy."

I really don't care what it is as long as it is healthy, Aj mused as she watched Leon's animated elation, and I am going to have a normal delivery. Look at Leon, he is so excited. He's having his first boy and he gets to name it after him and his dad to continue their legacy. My son is going to be the third, this is super awesome! Now I can start shopping and getting my son's room together.

Before Aj and Leon could leave the facility, they were both on their cell phones calling their families. They took great joy in letting them know that they were having a boy. Aj's mom always had grandmother fever, Mabel always wanted a grandchild and now she was finally getting one. Her father, Allen, was extremely proud as he anxiously awaited meeting his new grandson.

By the time Aj was seven months pregnant, the baby's room was almost fully furnished, and she happily awaited her trip to Milwaukee for the baby shower. Her best friend and baby sister put it all together. They limited who received an invitation, not everyone in the family was invited, as the day was to be all about celebrating a new life and no hard feelings were welcomed. Unfortunately, her mother, Mabel, tried time and again to change her mind and negate her feelings and therefore Aj kept her conversations with her mother as brief as possible.

"I'll talk to you later Mom, the baby has me worn out," Aj said sweetly.

"You know it's not right to exclude family from your baby shower," Mabel threw in.

"It's my baby shower and I don't want to have to go off on anybody that's not supposed to be there," Aj stated emphatically. "This is more so directed towards Ron, even though I really don't want Aunt Nancy to come either, but she can be an exception," Aj concluded.

"I will just tell Nancy that no men are allowed," Mabel said passively.

"Why can't you tell her the truth?"

"I'm just going to give it to God, and you should too."

"Goodbye Mom."

&

The morning of the baby shower dawned. Aj ran around still trying to get errands done for herself. She made an appointment to get her makeup done, as she wanted to be flawless for the pictures. The baby shower started at two p.m., although the poorest people were on CPT time. The event was held in the recreation room of Aj's grandmother's building.

Shana and Leah greeted everyone who arrived while Aj was upstairs getting dressed. Aj wanted to make an entrance after enough people arrived. Shana informed Aj when to come downstairs via text. Aj made her way to the party beaming with joy all the way. When she arrived, she was embraced by so many family members her heart filled with love and happiness.

I haven't seen some of my relatives in years. I can't believe they showed up. I'm so excited to see everyone. As happy as Aj was she could not stave off the fear that Ron would ruin her party with his presents: If Ron show up hell's going to break loose. He cannot be a part of my new life. I need to stop thinking about that pedophile. Aj looked around at her loving family and calmed her mind. Ron will not spoil this day for me, she concluded and refused to give her childhood tormentor another thought.

Shana conducted the baby shower games, and everyone participated. The family came together and truly celebrated the new life that Aj carried. They ate, drank, and had a great time. Leah designed a backdrop for people to stand in front of and take pictures. Leon's family showed up from Chicago including his sister and cousins with their kids who Aj had met before. It is really great seeing them all again, Aj thought, one of Leon's cousins is pregnant as well. I have an idea.

"We have to take pictures together with your pregnant belly and mine," Aj suggested.

"Yes definitely, a cousins' before birth picture," she agreed. "I heard you are having a boy, due in October. Congratulations!"

"Thank you! Yes, Leon the third. What about you?"

"I am having a girl and I'm due in December."

"Congratulations to you too, we're only like a couple of months apart."

"Thank you!"

"You're welcome. I'll be right back I need to talk to Shana's husband to get the photos arranged. He is the photographer."

Aj looked around the room and took in the pure joy of the party. Her family members and friends took pictures with their cell phones. She spotted the photographer and pulled him to the side.

"Please take pictures of everyone so I can have some professional pictures for myself," Aj asked. "People have camera phones, but I want the real deal."

"I've got you."

"Thank you."

This baby shower is so amazing: the colors are blue and gold; there was a treat table with decorated pretzels, rice crispy treats, candy jars; everyone is happy and getting along; and no Ron and Nancy, Aj mused. All the kids are going to have a stomachache especially once they eat some cake and ice cream, she laughed to herself.

The time came to open the gifts, and it was a nice number of gifts, Aj's already full heart overflowed with happiness as everything was greatly appreciated, and she thank everyone for every item.

"We have a lot to take back with us," Leon said.

"Just more stuff to add to our luggage," Aj replied merrily.

Once the baby shower was over Leon and Aj went to her aunt Coco's house to rest. They were scheduled to leave the next morning to go to Chicago to see Leon's parents before they headed back to Arizona. Aj sat on the couch in the living room with Coco.

CHAPTER SEVEN DADDY'S LITTLE GIRL

After the baby shower, Aj was the happiest she had ever been in the City of Milwaukee. This is what a normal life feels like, she mused as she basked in the love of her family and reveled in the sheer joy of her new life. For the first time since she was eleven years old, Ron did not steal her joy. Little did Aj know, her own aunts would cut into her like Jack the Ripper and rob her of her happiness; and that in the end, her very happy day and the remainder of her trip would be filled with trying conversations about the man who molested her as a child.

After a short time, Coco received an excess of text messages. The alerts came in so fast it sounded like it was a continuous ring tone. Aj took notice.

"What's going on Aunt Coco?" Aj asked curious.

"I'm in a group message with your mom, grandmother, Nancy and Lynn."

"What is this about?"

"Ron and Nancy weren't invited to the baby shower. Apparently, someone told her that there were no men allowed."

"I never said that there were no men allowed. Ron just wasn't invited. Why would I say that? My dad and brothers were there. Leon was there."

"A picture was posted on social media with you, Leon and his cousins, so Lynn took a screenshot of the picture and created the message for everyone."

"So, apparently my mom told Aunt Nancy no men were allowed to spare her feelings, but she didn't tell anyone the real reason why he couldn't come," Aj looked disgusted as she continued, "because he used to touch me as a kid."

Coco shook her head, as there was nothing she could say; after all Coco knew the truth from the beginning and chose to keep it from Nancy as well. The text messages chimed out of control and before long Coco started in on Aj. Aj barely had a moment to relax after the baby shower when the family drama was kicked up to the max.

"Aj you need to sit down with Nancy and have a conversation with her," Coco insisted.

"I don't want to talk about this tonight. Can't you see I'm happy with my new life? Can't I have today be all about me and my baby, my new family?"

"All I'm saying is…" Nancy started.

"What Aunt Coco?" Aj looked unflinchingly into Coco's eyes as she continued. "I was wrong for not wanting the child molester who for three years: sexually stalked me, tormented me with inappropriate touches, snuck up from behind me every chance he got so he could kiss me on the back of my neck and whisper the sick sex acts he wanted to do to me in my ear, and I firmly believe would have raped me if I didn't do everything I could to protect *myself*, at my baby shower?"

"Nancy should have been there," Coco asserted.

"She was invited," Aj said with a smirk. "Ron could not come. If Aunt Nancy cannot show up to one family function without her pedophile husband by her side, that's her problem not mine. He is not welcome in my new life."

"It is time for you to tell that to Nancy," Coco finished and excused herself for the remainder of the evening.

The next morning, before Aj headed out to go to Chicago, she sent a text message to Nancy. Maybe it is time for Aunt Nancy to hear the truth from my lips, she thought as she stared at the message screen. Everybody else seems to want to add their own spin, ok here goes.

Aj: I would like to meet so we can talk.

Nancy: You are a liar and that stuff you're saying didn't happen. You are delusional and a devil in sheep's clothing. You're always causing messy situations. All this because my husband kissed you on the cheek and you want to make up all these lies about my husband you need to seek professional help like go see a psychiatrist or something and lose my number don't ever contact me again and don't ever speak to my daughters lose their numbers too quit trying to destroy a happy home because your love life is messed up. Why did you come to my house and sit on my couch and used my address for stuff?

Aj: When I was a little girl, he was always in my face but after I was an adult he was never around. He stayed in y'all's basement most of the time. I tried for years to let it go, but I couldn't. What he did to me was wrong. I have no reason to lie and you can't shut me up.

Aj remembered a time, about a year before she moved to Arizona, when Nancy was in the hospital giving birth to her third daughter. Her oldest two daughters, seventeen-year-old Niyah, and Nia, who was about to turn thirteen, where home alone with their father, Ron, when Nia caught Ron in the bed with her big sister. The situation was brought up to Nancy that Ron had inappropriately touched his own daughter, in her bed. Nancy made threats and said that she was ready to get a divorce and call the police on her husband. She made such a big fuss yet took no action. The drama Nancy created put the fear of God into Nia. She was scared of being blamed for the breakup of her family. She was afraid of sending her father to jail and therefore she told her mom it was all a lie just to keep everyone under the same roof.

It is simply amazing, when I brought up the fact that Ron is a child molester, I'm such a liar and a delusional person, Aj fumed quietly. Nancy pretends to think her husband is so innocent and does no harm. She acts like she doesn't know Nia was telling the truth. I don't believe that for a minute. She knows the truth and bullied her own daughter into changing her story.

Aj: I will continue to tell my truth Aunt Nancy.

Aj's mind raced: And one day so will your daughters. Daddy's little girl has a dark, twisted meaning in your household Aunt Nancy. I wonder if being molested by her father made your daughter embrace lesbianism or was she born to it? I know what demons I have had to fight. I can't imagine if it was my own father who… Oh my God, if Ron was caught in the bed with Niyah, I hate to think of the years of abuse which led up to it. Nancy left her daughters alone with that sycophant all of the time. He must have started touching Niyah after he did what he did to Melanie. And I know he did that to Melanie just to get even with Aunt Coco. Aunt Coco should have just told Aunt Nancy the truth about Ron, because her lie protected the very child molester who defiled both of their daughters. Who's texting me now?

Allen: What is this stuff Ron's talking about on social media?

Aj: I haven't seen it Daddy.

Allen (Ron, screenshot): People need to let stuff go that happened fifteen years ago. It's old now.

Aj: I'll call you once I get to my destination Daddy.

Allen: Okay, I love you.

There was an attachment to the text message. Apparently, Ron in-boxed Allen and said your daughter is the devil. Aj read the message and smirked as she thought: What needs to be let go if NOTHING happened? That coward cannot admit what he did fifteen years ago but now people need to let it go because it is old news, really? Ron and my dad haven't spoken in years and yet, suddenly, he wants to reach out in a private message. I know he is feeling guilty.

Ron tried to reason with Allen. Aj's dad told her that Ron sent message after message after message on social media. Allen never messaged Ron back.

Aj and Leon met up with Leah for breakfast in downtown Milwaukee. It was Aj's favorite place to go every time she was in town. Once seated, Aj received a message from her grandmother.

Granny: Can you stop by before y'all hit the highway?

Aj: Sure, I'll call you when I'm done eating.

The waiter walked up to the table and took their orders. Leah ordered from the kid's menu because she was not going to eat much. Aj, Leon, and Leah laughed and had a great conversation as they waited for the waiter to return. Once their food was served, their server addressed Leah.

"I didn't know that was for you," the waiter said.

"What are you talking about?" Leah replied.

"I thought the kid's plate was for somebody else. I can get in trouble."

"Damn are you the food police? Watch out, move back I'm trying to eat!"

Aj just laughed because it was so funny. After all, there were no children with them when they sat down or when they ordered. Who else could the meal be for?

The time came to say their goodbyes. "I'll catch you later," Aj said as she and Leah hugged each other tight.

Aj got in the car and called her grandmother.

"Hello?"

"Hey Grandma, I'm on my way."

"Oh," was all she said before the phone hung up.

Grandma only lived five minutes away from thc restaurant. They pulled up, and Aj got out of the car alone. Leon chose to stay in the car. She went into her grandmothers building anticipating the worse. I have a feeling I know what she wants to talk about, but I'll wait till she brings it up, Aj thought. She did not have to wait long.

"What's going on? How come Ron wasn't invited to the baby shower?" Virginia asked the moment she answered the door.

"I can't let this man be a part of my happiness!" Aj replied as she walked into her grandmother's apartment. "He doesn't get to celebrate with me Grandma," Aj replied in earnest.

"Honey you got to let this go and go get some help. Why would you want to break up his family?"

"Excuse me? Are you serious? Can't nobody tell me what this man did to me only him and I know what happened. Of course, he's going to deny it."

"I don't have much money. Here go twenty-five dollars."

What's this for?"

"Just because," she said plainly.

You just told me at the baby shower you didn't have anything to give me, but now mysteriously, you've got twenty-five dollars. Almost seems like she was trying to buy my silence but I'm taking it anyways, Aj mused. Is this what she and her husband did to shut her daughter up?

"Thank you, Grandma, I have to go. I'll see you later."

Aj left, as she walked away she thought: I need to hurry up and get back in the car, so we can finally get on the road to head to Chicago because Leon has to see his family too. As soon as she got in the car she went straight to sleep, tired as ever and fed up with all the bull crap going on in her family. While napping she heard her phone blowing up nonstop. She just told herself: I'll return those calls once I wake up, they can wait.

The drive was two hours long. After they made it to Chicago Aj thought of her dad. I did tell my dad I was going to call him back. He wants to know what Ron was posting on social media was all about. I can do this, Aj reflected, it's time.

Aj took deep breath and called her dad. She was a little scared and very nervous to finally have the most difficult conversation, thus far in her life, with her father.

"Daddy, when I was a little girl, Aunt Nancy's husband, Ron, used to come up behind me and touch me inappropriately," Aj began. She was brave and very candid as she divulged the woes of her childhood torture, at Ron's pedophilic hands, to her daddy. She tried her level best not to cry but this was her dad. This was the first time she felt strong enough to ever tell him. He quietly listened, without judgment or blame until she had spoken the final word of her truth.

"I just wished you told me back when I was a police officer," Allen said, pain reverberated in his voice as he continued, "I could have done something, or put him in jail."

"I know Daddy, I was just too scared to say something, and he always told me don't tell nobody which I never did until it happened at Aunt Coco's house. Mama and Aunt Coco twisted my words against me, switched up the story and made me apologize to Aunt Nancy. So, I just kept my mouth shut after that, I didn't tell anyone else in the family."

"This is the reason why he keeps messaging me. Ron is trying to reason with me. He keeps sending me message after message after message on social media. He is probably scared out his mind."

"He should be," Aj stated.

"The next step I want you to do is call down to the police station and see what options you have," Allen began gallantly, "You should also consider suing for pain and suffering."

"Thank you, Daddy. You are the only member of the family to take my side in this."

"You are my daughter, my first-born baby girl. It is my job to protect you."

"Let me do some research and I'll call you back."

"I love you, goodbye."

"I love you too Daddy."

The next call came from Lynn, however Aj looked at the call screen and chose not to answer. She was lost in thought as she waited for the ringing to stop: She is jealous of me and always has been, even when I was a little girl. I was too pretty, my daddy loved me too much, the hate was undeniable. Now that I am an adult I will not tolerate it. Lynn was the one who started this whole thing, all the way from Florida. What, I was too happy, so you had to cause problems? Don't be mad at me because my life is better than yours. Good, no voicemail, one less thing I have to erase.

Aj deleted Lynn off her social media pages and removed her aunt's number from her phone. Goodbye Aunt Lynn, you are irrelevant to me, a non-factor. You would think my family would have my back, but it seems like most of my mom's sisters are siding with Ron, who's married into the family. When I would have conversations with my cousins they always say, "All he does is stare. He is a creep." I'm thinking that I'm the only one who said something. Then again I can't imagine who I could have confided in had my own daddy climbed into bed on top of me. I can't imagine the psychological demons my little cousin must be dealing with. Although I feel bad for what happened to Melanie, I feel sorry for you Niyah. Hopefully, one day, Melanie and Niyah will find the courage to tell their truth.

Aj got out the car and went into Leon's mom house. They were only going to be in Chicago for a day before they headed to Arizona. August in Milwaukee was wintery, and Chicago's weather was not any better.

I can't wait to get back to some sunshine and ninety-degree weather, Aj pondered; I can't do this cold no more, this is one of the reasons why I'm not back in the Midwest. I hate being cold. It is nice and warm in here. Thank you for having the heat on.

Aj enjoyed her visit with Leon's mother. She embraced Aj at hello and welcomed her into the family with open arms. Aj was happy again, as her new life had budded nicely with her new family.

"Mama, it's time for Aj and I to go visit the rest of the family," Leon said.

Leave me here," Aj interjected. "I don't want to go back in the cold plus I'm pregnant too and comfortable. Nah, I'm good. Tell them to come by here.

"Woman is you crazy? My momma don't want all them people in her house."

"Hellllllllll," Aj began, "but I'm not getting out the car."

❧

The following morning, Aj smiled as she ruminated: We are on our way to the airport, my favorite part of this trip, to go back to my new home. The flight is like three hours long. Bring on the warm Arizona sun.

Alas, their flight did not land until Sunday night. All they had time to do was go home, unpack, and get ready for work the next day. Aj and Leon settled in for a good night's rest. Unfortunately for Aj, the baby had other plans. Contractions started at eleven p.m. that night.

Worried, Leon asked, "Do you want to go to the emergency room?"

"Yes, let's go."

Aj and Leon were exhausted on the twenty-minute drive to the hospital. All Aj wanted to do was sleep, however, the contractions were kicking her butt. Aj had the foresight to pre-register, so they would not have to ask a lot of questions however they still ended up asking them anyway before they sent her back. The doctor checked Aj.

"You are dilated one centimeter," the doctor said and Aj's jaw just dropped.

"Really that's it?" she asked.

"At this point there's nothing much we can really do because your water hasn't broken yet. We are going to send you home to progress further."

Aj was very irritated as she thought: When you come home in the middle of the night from the hospital after thinking that you are in labor and all you want to do is go to sleep because I do have to wake up at six thirty in the morning to go to work, but the contractions are keeping you up…

The alarm went off far too soon for Aj's taste. She went into work a little late because she was simply exhausted. While she worked contractions plagued her. Braxton Hicks contractions felt more real as her day progressed. Aj was determined to hold off returning to the emergency department, in fact, she stuck it out all day. Her shift came to an end. Leon picked her up from work and took her home.

"I just want to take a nice hot bath and just relax," Aj said as she entered her home.

Aj lit a candle and relaxed in the tub for at least an hour while she listened to some jazz music. After her bath she enlisted Leon to help her get out of the tub, as it was too hard for her to get out by herself and she did not want to trip getting out and risk hurting her baby. The bath was exactly what she needed as she dried off and fell asleep on her stomach.

"Get up your squishing him," Leon said as he nudged Aj awake.

"I want to sleep on my stomach so bad," Aj responded sleepily as she rolled onto her side. "He's protected in the sack Leon. I'm tossing and turning all night with these contractions," her voice trailed off as sleep overtook her again.

Aj's water broke at two forty-one in the morning. She was shocked awake as the water gushed out. She immediately woke Leon.

"My water broke," Aj stated half panicked.

Leon went back to sleep, as Aj's words did not register. She hit him in the back and told him louder that her water broke. He finally got up. While she got dressed, Leon packed two or three outfits for her hospital stay.

"Where do you think I am going," Aj asked. "Let's go now."

Aj was too lazy to pack a bag as she just wanted to get out of there. Nevertheless, they took at least ten minutes before they finally left the house, at which point she was ready to slap him because he was doing too much. Aj sent a text to her mom first, then her manager and told them her water broke and she was on her way to the hospital. She called her friend Shannon.

"Hello," Shannon answered,

"I am on my way to the hospital," Aj said as she breathed through a contraction.

"I'm on my way," Shannon replied with a quickness. "I'll meet you there."

Shannon had been one of Aj's greatest friends since she lived in Arizona. She was very loyal and honest. Shannon was more like family.

Once Aj and Leon arrived at the hospital, they took her back right away. To her chagrin, they asked Aj the same questions as they had done two times before; once when she pre-registered and again the night before.

"I was just here last night don't you have the information already?" Aj asked

"We have to do this every time."

What's the point of pre-registering then?"

Leon interceded, "Calm down now, please."

"How, when these contractions are kicking my butt?" asked AJ.

They took Aj to the delivery room to get more comfortable and gave her some pain medicine. Shannon arrived moments later. Before long Aj no longer felt the contractions as much, although she became even sleepier. All she wanted to do was take a nap to save some energy for when it came time for her to push. Shannon had to leave to go back to work. Hours and hours went by and the baby did not come out. Finally, the nurse gave Aj a ball to put between her legs to help the process.

"If you feel like there is certain pain in your cervix press the button," the nurse said.

"Okay," Aj replied.

Before the nurse could make it back to the nurse's station Aj was pressing that button like forty going north. The birthing team rushed in her room.

The nurse said, "Okay he's coming!"

Amazingly enough, Shannon made it back to the hospital just in time to see the baby come out, as he was out after only three pushes. Leon the third was six pounds, thirteen ounces, and nineteen inches long. When Aj got to hold him in her arms, it was tears of joy as she always wanted to be a mother.

"I feel strange, something isn't right," Aj said.

Shannon went over to her and asked, "What's wrong?

"I don't want to die."

"What are you talking about?"

"I see the white light. I don't want to die."

"Girl you are not going to die."

Aj passed out. During the delivery, the baby had torn the perineum and the posterior vaginal wall. There was so much blood. The doctor stopped the bleeding and stitched her up. Everyone thought Aj had made it through the worse. Shannon called the nurse over. The nurse put an ammonia capsule under her nose in an attempt to get her to wake up, however it did not work, and therefore she tried another one. Aj came to, finally. Her blood pressure was seventy-four over forty-four, almost in stroke mode, however, her determination was 100%.

I need to live! I have to enjoy my son. He needs his mother. I'm not done with life yet. There is so much stuff I need to do and accomplish. I have to be here, I have to!

Slowly but surely, Aj's blood pressure went up. The nurse left the room and ran some tests. After being gone for a while the nurse returned.

"You need a blood transfusion," the nurse said.

"No, I decline, because I have heard so many things about how people come in contact with all these diseases from blood transfusions."

"Blood transfusions are perfectly safe."

"Let me think about it."

"Okay, I'll check with you tomorrow."

The next day Aj was in the recovery room where visitors were allowed. Aj got up and took a shower. She looked in the mirror and saw how pale and yellow she was. She said to herself, "Okay I'll get the transfusion, so I can get a jump start back to great health." She pressed the button for the nurse to come. The nurse entered the room.

"What can I do for you Ms. Rashond?"

"I've changed my mind. I want the blood transfusion."

"Wonderful, I have to order two bags for you, and because you need that much blood and the state laws, it is going to take about two hours."

The nurse left and shortly thereafter, Leon left to go pick up Aj's mom from the airport to bring her to the hospital. Aj was finally able to get on her phone. There were so many missed calls and voicemails. She started with the voicemails. The first was a message from a shipping company saying they delivered the baby's bed.

Aj thought, I'll call back and tell them off. How do you leave a baby bed on the front porch if no one was at home? You should have taken it to the front desk of the apartment complex. I'll call Leon and tell him once he drops my mom off here, to go to the house and put the baby bed inside the apartment. These fools left it outside.

There was a knock on the door. Aj put down her phone and looked up as the door opened. Her friend Tanya stopped by to see her and the baby. During her visit with Tanya, Mabel finally arrived. She was super excited to be with her first grandchild, to hold him in her arms, but she patiently waited for Tanya to put him down.

"I have to go back to work," Tanya said. "I'll be by the house later to see him."

"Come to Grandma," Mabel cooed. Aj's mother picked up the baby. She did not want to put him down. "Look at my handsome grandson."

After Aj's blood transfusion her energy returned and so did her color. Unfortunately, she had to stay in the hospital for another night, as she looked forward to sleeping in her own bed. That night she was excited as finally she slept on her stomach. She laid her hospital bed all the way back and stretched out. I haven't done this in a long time, she thought happily before she nodded off to sleep.

Morning came, and baby Leon woke up hungry. AJ prepared him a bottle, because she still waited for her breast to fill up with milk. The nurse came down with discharge papers and said that she could leave. Aj put her clothes on with a quickness. Leon went and got the car pulled around.

There was no separating Aj's mother from her very first grandson. In fact, Mabel ended up staying for about a week, to help out with the baby. Aj having to go back to work was the perfect excuse she needed to stay on. After Mabel departed, Leon was on morning duty and Aj took night duty since she was a night owl.

❧

Shortly after baby Leon turned six months old, Aj told her family that she would bring him to Milwaukee. Her goal was to allow her son to get used to her brothers, sisters, cousins, and the rest of the family. They ended up staying at her mother's house, although normally Aj would get a hotel. This trip was special and Aj did not want to offend anyone.

People always think you're bougie when you stay at a hotel or think there's something wrong with their house if you refuse to stay with them, Aj thought as Leon and she got settled in. It's going to be a long weekend. I have events that I have to attend, and my son has to go with me to all of them.

"Aj," Mabel called out as she entered the room. "Can I take baby Leon over to Nancy and Ron's house because Nancy wants to see her great nephew?"

"Are you asking for Ron to get shot? Hell nah! He isn't going over there. Ron probably likes little boys too. If she wants to see him she can come over here. My son is never going over there. You must be smoking to even ask me that."

Nancy never stopped by to see her great nephew. Eventually, Coco stopped by and then other family members went over as well. They asked Aj about her experiences with motherhood thus far and they wanted to know when she and baby Leon would visit next. Mabel suggested they return for his first birthday as the majority of the family lived there in

Milwaukee and only the three of them lived in Arizona. Aj agreed.

CHAPTER EIGHT
WHY NOW?

Baby Leon's big birthday was fast approaching. Almost one-year of motherhood and Aj could not have been happier. Her son was turning one year old and her sister was planning his party. Leah figured since the baby's name was Leon the birthday party should be ninja turtle theme, although Aj really wanted it to be lion king. As it turned out it was difficult for Aj to find lion king décor and party favors. She guessed it was no longer in style. Leah created the invitations and sent them out to people. She also created an event on social media, since most of the family connected there, and invited them via evite.

Aj in-boxed Nancy and Ron's daughter, Niyah, her first cousin, on social media and informed her personally of her son's birthday party. Niyah replied one week later.

Niyah: With all due respect please don't contact me you have something against my dad smh...

Aj: Just thought the little babies can come together to meet but it's not your fault you're getting the wrong information when you're ready for the truth hit me up there's two sides to every story.

Niyah: Bullshit!! So, what's the truth Andrea?

Aj: No need for cuss words ma'am were both grown I've never done nothing to you, so the truth was your dad use to touch me inappropriately when I was little and all it did was get swept under the rug, I have no need to lie about anything that does nothing for me why make this up.

Niyah: Okay so first of all my dad never touched you. When did he have time to do that shit Aj? When have you ever been alone with him? SMH That's crazy as fuck that you would just now say this last year when it supposedly happened what seventeen, eighteen years ago... Just because he gave you hugs, and shit don't mean he touched you. You really broke up the family for some bullshit like this... I'm a just say this if you got a problem with my dad you got a problem with me cause at the end of the day, I'mma always have his side... So, if he can't be around because of yo sick fantasy then me and my daughter can't either.... Sorry

Aj: It's ok if you don't want to believe no one ever do and if the family broke up not my problem but my truth was my truth and can't nobody tell me that he didn't so I know what happen and that's all that matters of course you're going to believe your dad I mean it's your dad who wants to hear those things about their father so we don't have to speak it's crazy how everybody's in denial.

Niyah: I don't believe you SMH that shit crazy ass fuck. Don't nobody believe you. Like I said since you got a problem with my dad you got one with me as well like... you need help go talk to someone.

Gee, I am not going through this anymore, Aj thought and stopped replying. Niyah is just as ignorant as her momma. Besides, according to Nia, Niyah needs more help than I do. Wow, her own dad.

Aj was at home packing a bag for baby Leon and one for herself, in preparation for their trip to Milwaukee. She picked up her phone and scrolled through the posts on social media. She read a post from Melanie which stated that their grandmother wanted to have a family meeting at her house. Moments later, Aj's phone rang.

"Hello grandma," Aj greeted happily.

"I want a family meeting," Virginia began straight away. "Here at my house on Saturday. Everyone needs to be there."

"My son's party is on Saturday, so I won't have time, and besides what's this about anyway," Aj asked.

"Hey, you just make it here."

"I will be there tonight."

"Where you at now?"

"I'm getting ready to go to the airport."

"Oh, girl thought you was already here."

"No not yet. I'm looking forward to that sweet potato pie so, have it ready."

"Where you at, home? I have nothing for you yet. I have to go to the store. I don't know if I can go get them today."

"Okay Grandma let me finish getting ready. Big Leon is waiting to take us to the airport."

"Hold on one minute, you getting ready, I can't keep you from getting ready," Virginia stated before she asked, "Big Leon flying out tomorrow?"

"He's dropping me and baby Leon off today."

"How come y'all not coming together?"

"He's flying into Chicago because he has to pick his parents up."

"Oh, you flying into Milwaukee, ok. Let me tell you what's going on," she carried on. "This a family thing and I want us all to be together to come to the party: kids, great grandkids. I was chatting with Niyah and I invited her, and she said you got a problem with her dad, you got a problem with her, so she's not coming."

"Okay whatever, Saturday I'm going to be running around trying to get stuff ready for the party…"

Virginia interrupted, "She know that you don't want Ron to come."

"No, I don't want him there," Aj stated adamantly.

"You're not going to change your mind?"

"No grandma! I can't have somebody that harmed me still be invited to my son's party. I just can't do that."

"Well she think y'all should have talked about it. You should have went and got some help. He been in the family for years and you know he isn't going nowhere."

"I mean, he shouldn't have been in the family that's the thing. As soon as they found out he should have been kicked out the family."

"That's Nancy husband so she not going to do anything, if you don't want him there that's you. She know you and your sister going to be doing a lot of running around she was just saying you could change your mind and y'all can talk about it so everybody can show up there. I don't like for nobody to be really left out and that's the only son in law that I have right? He shouldn't be…

"I feel like once y'all knew what this man done shouldn't nobody talk to him. I don't have support from this family, like why do he get to come around to everything when people know he was a pedophile?"

"Well who knows he's a pedophile though," Grandmother asked doubtful.

"I told people he was," Aj answered courageously.

"You shouldn't be going around telling people that, just drop it and leave it alone,"

"I can't drop it."

"You can't say he was a pedophile if he ain't talk to nobody but you or looked at nobody but you," Aj's grandmother habitually defended the child molester.

"But he touched me inappropriately..." Aj's voice trailed off.

"I don't know what you mean," Virginia lied, "That's alright, we'll talk about it another time," she dismissed Aj.

"When I say he touched me inappropriately," Aj continued on, as she refused to have her truth set aside. "I'm not talking about a kiss or a hug. When I was a kid he used to come behind me and touch and rub on me. He would kiss on my neck and say vile things to me. Ron would press his privates against my backside."

"Him and Nancy have always been together. How could this happen when nobody was around?"

"Do you think I'm making this up?"

"Well where was we at, you mean to tell me he sneaked out from everybody to come find you?"

"Yes, he did. He didn't care! When he used to come over to shoot darts and play pool with my dad, he would act like he was going to the bathroom just to try to find me. The thing is, I don't have to lie."

"Don't say no more! I don't want to hear it just drop it!" Grandmother chided. "That's ok, just get your baby ready, and tell Melanie to cancel the meeting."

Wow, Grandma is against me too, Aj considered. The gravity of her own grandmother, the most loveable woman Aj had known, turning her back on the truth was staggering. "Don't say no more! I don't want to hear it just drop it!" echoed in Aj's mind. You don't want to hear how Ron had everybody fooled? Okay, no problem, but you will not stop me from telling my truth!

Hours later, Aj arrived at the airport. She got checked in and patiently waited in line at security with a fussy baby in her arms. As she headed up to board the plane she got a call from Coco.

"What happen between you and Niyah?"

"That girl was so disrespectful after I told her what her dad used to do to me. The whole point was for her to bring her daughter, but then it went sideways."

"You'd have to go over to Nancy and Ron's house to see what's going on," Coco stated. "I told Nancy that the only people who know what happened were Ron and you. I want you to know that Nancy is planning on getting an attorney because you're supposedly slandering her husband's name and they are trying to sue you."

"Only guilty people get lawyers but let them bring it because they are going to lose." Aj declared triumphantly. "I'm boarding my plane now. I'll call when I touched down."

The flight was three hours long and therefore, Aj wanted to get all settled in on the plane and maybe even take a nap as baby Leon was finally knocked out. The flight was smooth sailing from beginning to end. Aj sent a text to her sister that told her they had landed, and they would be ready in about twenty minutes. Aj had to wait to get their luggage.

I hate traveling with so many bags, Aj fumed. I have the stroller, car seat, his diaper bag, my purse and suitcase, this was too much. My back is hurting and all. I didn't get no sleep on the plane… Too much on my mind to rest… I hate having to fight against my own family because some grown ass man, a sick SOB, decided he was sexually attracted to little girls.

Great! Leah has finally arrived. They loaded the car up and took off down the road. It is cold as hell here, and my son is not used to this weather. He's used to onesies and shorts, not long sleeves shirts and pants with coats but I must bundle him up. I don't want him to get sick because of this weather difference, Aj pondered.

They arrived at Leah's house, Mabel, lived with her daughter. As soon as they got in the door, Mabel was just so excited to see baby Leon; except for the fact he was asleep. With the two-hour time difference, his sleep pattern was going to be all messed up, especially when he goes to bed at a certain time, Aj considered. I have to get settled in because my sister and I have a busy day tomorrow. We have a lot of running around to do and still have to get stuff for the party.

The next morning Leah had to go to work. Aj and baby Leon dropped her off and headed back to the house to try to get some sleep. I'm tired as heck and didn't sleep well last night but that comes with being out of town, Aj thought, I want to visit my family but I'm going to see them at the party, which was best because people can't say I didn't come by to visit them with baby Leon.

Hours later, a well rested Aj and her son Leon went to Coco's house. She took a shower and got dressed for the party. I don't have to pick Leah up from work; thank God she is getting dropped off over here. It is too cold for baby Leon to go outside, Aj thought as she finished applying her makeup.

Coco's house was to be the meet up spot for the cousins to stop by the night before the party to talk and have drinks. Melanie, Siyah, and Marie, arrived one after the other. It's been a minute since we all hung out, Aj mused. I'm so excited to hang out with my family. Aj's cousin from Chicago, Shelia, and her son showed up as well. Once Leah arrived Aj looked at her sister and smiled. She thought, this is nice thank you Leah. They all drank, laughed, and caught up on each other's lives.

Aj, Leah, and baby Leon headed out, as the next day was Leon's big birthday party and they still had a lot of running around to do. They picked up their brother Alani from the bus station, he was a college student and he wanted to come to the party as well. They all went to the store and grabbed the rest of the food for the party, at least forty people were expected. They returned to Leah's house, unloaded the groceries, sat at the kitchen table, and put together candy bags for the party.

"I booked a photo session for baby Leon's first birthday pictures," Leah said. "I booked it at nine a.m., in the morning."

"That's early as hell to get up on a Saturday," Aj laughed.

"Yes, however you get same day pictures, which takes about thirty minutes to an hour to get."

"Good point, thank you for everything Leah."

The next morning Aj, Leah, and Baby Leon were on their way bright and early. There were smiles all around during the photo session and after. Once the proofs were loaded, Aj and Leah sat down together and perused.

"Baby Leon did so well taking the pictures, he's a natural." Aj commented with a proud grin.

"He is handsome," Leah agreed.

This day was already starting off great, Aj considered.

Once the photo shoot was done, they went to the house. They carefully put the party stuff in the car. Aj got a call from Siyah.

"I spoke to Grandma and she was pretty much telling me that if Ron was not coming to the party then she won't be coming to the party because we have to stop this, and she wants all her family to be in the same room."

"Well that's not going to happen. What part don't they understand? I said he's not welcomed?" Aj stated strongly. "So, Grandma is going to miss her great-grandson's first birthday because of a child molester, okay then." Aj's call waiting chimed. "Let me call you back, that's Marie." She clicked over, "Hello."

"Aj, my mom called me and asked me if you were telling the truth or not about what Ron did to you," Marie said.

"Really? Aunt Lynn asked you?"

"I told her if she wanted any information that she needed to contact you but before I could hang up the phone my mom asked me had Ron done anything to me, as if she was going to believe me."

"Right…"

It's crazy no one wants to believe me because I'm the niece but sometimes I do wonder if my aunts were told that Ron did touch their daughters would it be a different end result? Nancy didn't want to believe her own daughter although she had no reason to lie. She scared that girl into changing her story because she feared her family would break up and her father would go to jail. Yeah, that's what this family does. Scare us into being silent as children and then try to shame us into letting it go as adults. I'm just glad nothing happened to Marie.

The guy at the pavilion, where the party was to be held, called.

"You can come early to set up if you wanted to."

"Sure, I'm actually on the way right now."

They arrived at the pavilion shortly thereafter. They had the space decorated in no time at all. The party started at two thirty p.m., but people hardly ever came in time for events, however one by one they showed up. Shannon got the games going on for the kids. The games were all so creative which was why Aj put Shannon in charge of it. She did such amazing job. Big Leon and his mother arrived at the party. Aj noticed the moment her grandmother arrived.

I didn't think she was coming because Ron's not invited, which she made very clear. I don't know why she wants him to come so bad. I don't have very much to say to her or anybody that's team Ron. They might as well not talk to me because they're are sick in the head as well.

The party went off without a hitch. Baby Leon really enjoyed his party and the family really enjoyed baby Leon. The night wound down as the party came to an end.

"Wait everyone," Leah shouted, "Please give me a moment before y'all leave." Everyone stopped and turned. "I have an announcement, I am pregnant!"

Everyone was so shocked and happy, including Aj. Although Aj knew prior as her sister sent her a text one day while she was at work announcing her pregnancy, and that she was super excited and couldn't wait to be a mother. The family gathered around Leah and congratulated her before they headed out. Aj's grandmother didn't talk to her until it was time to go. Everyone was on their way out the door.

Aj held her happy baby boy in her arms and kissed his face before she put him in the car. The moment he settled into his car seat, he was knocked out. Since that night was their last day in Milwaukee, they all went by Coco's house again. They met up and all of their kids said bye to each other. Unfortunately, the whole time Aj thought her flight left in the evening at six pm when in fact, their departure was in the morning at six a.m.

"It's nine at night, your flight is at six in the morning, your plane boards at five forty-five a.m. and you're on standby," Big Leon informed Aj shortly after their arrival at Coco's house. "We're getting back on the road to Chicago in an hour."

"So, I know I'm not going to be here long. We got to go back to my sister's house to pack all these toys and clothes he got at his party."

It was four o'clock in the morning and of course Aj did not get any sleep as usual. They made it to the airport in time, they unloaded the car, got all of their stuff checked in, got themselves checked in, and just when they thought they made it through security, an overzealous agent decided to stop them.

Bad enough we are flying standby, which can be exhausting because you stand and watch everybody go by and nine times out of ten we don't get on the plane, Aj thought as she rolled her eyes and continued: The fun part is when you're through the TSA check and they want you to take all of your baby things off including his shoes, and then break down the car seat and stroller so it can go through the process.

Of course, they went through all of that extra security checking and the flight was fully booked. The next plane out was in eleven hours and there was no guarantee for sure there would be seats available.

"We can leave out from Chicago on Tuesday at six in the morning," Aj read her best choice out loud. "At this point I'm just so over this trip." Aj called her sister. "Could you come back and get us please." Aj paused. "You know what, never mind, I know you are pregnant and tired, so we'll just catch a cab back to your house."

"Okay," replied Leah.

Aj and the baby arrived back at Leah's house just after seven in the morning. Everyone was still sleeping. Aj called Shelia. All Aj wanted to do was get out of Milwaukee. Spending a day or two with Leon's family was much better than to fight with her own.

"Shelia, what time are you leaving out so we can ride back with you to Chicago?"

"I'm leaving at five p.m.," Shelia said.

"That's perfect, I can finally rest up."

Leah and Mabel cooked breakfast, after which, Aj rested for about four hours. Once she woke up she realized that she could not shower and change clothes because they had shipped her bags to Arizona. Shelia took Aj shopping, she purchased clothes for two days. They went to Shelia's aunt's house, she made dinner for them to take on the road. Aj could not wait to take hers back to Coco's house, so Aj ate her meal there. She was super hungry as she had not eaten since breakfast.

Finally, they said their goodbyes, went back to Coco's house, grabbed their things, and hit the highway. Sheila and Aj passed the time with conversations about past relationships, taking trips etc. As the hours passed on the road to Chicago, Sheila broached the subject of Ron.

"When we were at Coco's house, I heard what's going on between you, Ron, and Nancy," Sheila began timidly.

"What you think about what's going on?" Aj asked.

"What's your side of the story?"

"Ron touched me as a child."

"Why tell now?"

"Well, because I've been carrying this burden on my shoulders for a long time plus by him saying, don't tell no one, that stayed with me for over a decade. I mean I'm a grown woman and I still can't open my mouth. He doesn't get to have this kind of hold on me no more."

"I feel you."

"Can't nobody tell me what happen. They just don't want to accept the fact that it happened."

"So, they're mad at you because you don't want to share your child's first birthday with a pedophile?"

"Yes. My grandma said she wasn't even coming to baby Leon's birthday party because the family's only living child molester, as her husband is now dead, was not invited. She told me to drop it."

"Damn…" Shelia was so shocked, she could not believe it. She had a wow look plastered on her face.

❧

Coco created a group chat with Siyah, Shelia, Leah, Melanie and Aj where they all kept in contact with each other and uploaded pictures of their children. A lot of the time when messages came through, Aj did not respond because the messages pretty much pertained to the family in Milwaukee. Marie had a baby and her mother, Lynn, was in town. Everyone was supposed to go by Nancy and Ron's house to meet up, but everyone went to Marie's house instead. Siyah send Aj a private message:

Siyah: You should come by Marie house.

Siyah sure did want to start something, as she sent a laughing emojis, Aj thought although she replied:

Aj: Let them have they shine. They finally getting invited somewhere. When I have an event, they can't never come their whole family is band. I am so glad my new life does not include a child molester.

Aj's mind wondered for a moment: According to some of the family members they think this was all accusations and false information, but they know it's been said more than once but yet he still gets invited to all the family functions and it just upsets me, but I know I can't make people feel how I feel but dang he deserves to be under the jail.

CHAPTER NINE
KARMA

"You're delusional. Quit making up lies. No one believes you. You waited too long to tell. Where did the events supposedly happen? You can't call Ron a child molester if it only happened to you. I don't want to hear no more," voices echoed through Aj's mind. "Get help… Get help. Get help!"

After what I have been through with the family, I should write a book, Aj mused. She sat in the living room of her home and cradled her son in her arms. He smiled up at her just before he drifted off to sleep. Aj gently rocked baby Leon as she slowly crept to his room and laid him in his crib.

Months had passed since she and her son visited her family in Milwaukee, and yet the drama which resulted seemed to be never ending. All of the negative reactions aimed towards a young lady who was targeted by a child molester and dared to tell her truth, were meant to crush her spirit and finally shut her up. Little did her family know, all they succeeded in doing was spurring her on. The Grandmother who did not want to hear the truth, the mother who refused to support the truth, the aunt who changed the truth, the aunt who refused to believe the truth, and cousin who outright rejected the truth all inspired AJ to share her truth.

Aj went to her room, gathered pen and paper, and settled in at the kitchen table with a bottle of wine.

She poured herself a glass and smiled as she wrote: HE SAID DON'T TELL.

"Get help," they said. Okay then, I heard writing can be cathartic, so here I go. This is the first step in reclaiming my dignity. I shall face my childhood ignominy head on and prevail. I will address every instance, every family member who tried to discredit me or shut me up. I will write with all of my heart. I can only pray that someone reads my words and stands up for themselves; the sooner, the better.

I want to reach out to other individuals like me. I will step up and tell my truth right here, right now, no matter what, no matter who. I hope to inspire others to tell their truths as well. I want victims to know, they no longer have to be afraid. They do not have to hold the pedophile's dark secret inside, nor do they have to be alone, or keep to themselves.

I want the survivors of sexual child abuse to know: You are not the only one to which this travesty has happened. The pain, the shame, the indignity, and the self-loathing you endured when you were a little boy or girl was not your fault. Free yourself from the disgrace and stigmata by transferring the blame to where it really belongs, the sycophant who molested you.

Feeling inspired, Aj called all of her cousins. She asked everyone who answered, one by one, had they been victimized or molested, by word or touch, had they been sexually harassed, sexually stalked, or anything of that nature. She paced her apartment as she waited for each answer. She curled up on the couch as she spoke with Marie, peeked in on her son as she waited for her call to Niyah to go to voicemail, and she lay across her bed as she spoke with Siyah and Nia. They all said no except for one, Nancy and Ron's youngest daughter Nia

"I am in this program for young black achievers and the director is sexually harassing me," Nia confessed.

Aj sat up straight and asked, "Did you tell your parents?" She gripped the phone a little bit too hard as she listened.

"No, I'm just going to let the school handle it."

"I'm here for you Nia if there is anything I can do."

"Thank you Aj."

The called ended shortly thereafter. Aj lay back on the bed again as the past flooded into her mind and swarmed around.

If Nia tells her parents, how would they handle it? Would Nancy be so quick to call the police and have that person put in jail or would she think her daughter was lying. How would Ron react to some man sexually harassing his daughter? Would he even care? Does a child molester even know how to protect his or her own child?

I need to do some research into the mind of a child molester and into my own family history too. I have heard stories about my mother's stepfather however no one wants to talk about it. Maybe everyone knew what happened to my mother, maybe no one knows. I am not sure, but I am going to find out. Moreover, I need to come to terms with the why and how of what happened to me and my cousins.

Aj spent weeks researching the behavior patterns of child molesters. Every day after she put baby Leon down to bed she sat in the kitchen with her laptop, pen, and paper. The more she read the more at peace she became. As she took her time and compared the characteristics of pedophiles to every action Ron took point by point, the truth dawned on her and filled her heart with joy.

"I have nothing to feel ashamed of!" Aj shouted out with happiness. "There's nothing wrong with me," she continued with a self-affirming smile plastered on her face. "Ron is just a typical, paradigmatic, textbook, totally by the numbers, common, as basic as he can be pedophile."

1. Child molesters have the tendency to show an excessive interest in children. Ron was definitely the favorite uncle to the children under nine years old.

2. Pedophiles seduce children, gain their love and trust with attention, affection, and gifts. More than that, they work long and hard patiently at developing relationships with their chosen victim. Ron picked up all of the girls and spun them around and gave them money, even still he managed to make Aj feel like she was more special than the rest.

3. Child molesters are master manipulators, which is most effective on overlooked children. Child molesters build up the child's self-esteem and lure the child in by making the child feel seen, heard, understood, valued, and less alone. Ron often said for all to hear that Aj was his favorite. Ron gave Aj more money than anyone else.

4. Pedophiles are very charming and friendly, as their goal is to gain widespread trust, easy access, and free rein, no matter how much time it takes. Ron became best friends with a police officer, Allen, Aj's father, after she refused to return to Nancy and Ron's house for sleepovers.

5. Child molesters are very skillful at lying and manipulation. Ron often faked having to use the bathroom to seek out Aj in her own home with both of her parents right there in the house with them.

6. Children respect and obey adults, Pedophiles exploit status to influence and control a child's behavior. Ron told Aj not to tell. What happened in this house stays in this house.

7. Child molesters seek out lonely, neglected, shy, quiet, naïve, children. They manipulate children to stay close to them. Ron gave Aj money to write him thank you letters. She was the oldest girl and relied on school friends for companionship. Ron said it hurt his feelings when Aj no longer wanted to be his favorite niece.

8. Pedophiles often test their intended victims. They stand physically too close for comfort, hug much too long, accidentally on purpose touch inappropriately, and/or make suggestive comments. Ron stood behind Aj and touched her as often as he could get away with it. Ron asked a thirteen-year-old child to let him suck her breasts.

9. Child molesters often claim to be misunderstood or joking when they get caught. The moment Coco confronted Ron he claimed to be playing around with Aj, just joking.

10. A pedophile makes his victim feel so special that the victim feels jealousy when they learn of other victims. Niyah became really angry and defensive when Aj told her the truth about her father, yet, Nia Ron's other daughter who caught her daddy in bed with Niyah, did not get upset, hmmm?

Aj read over her notes and shook her head, as she thought: A child molester needs to feel like they are in control and therefore they choose children to dominate, because they have no control or power in their own lives. When a man has his will subverted by a woman he seeks to find something or someone over which he can exert his will completely, that cannot resist him. Ron was out for revenge against Nancy because she subverted his whole life, she was in control, or so she thought. Poor Niyah, she must have thought she was special, when all along she was just the only girl left. Ron knew Nia was not an option because she would tell.

I need to call mom. She was sexually touched by her stepdad and she never really told anyone, after her mom said she did not believe her.

"Hello," Mabel answered.

"Hey Mom, I am writing a book and it would be nice to add other women stories in my book, so these women can know they are not alone and its ok to step forward."

"I let God handle all that," replied Mabel.

"I'll talk to you later Mom."

Aj was lost in thought: Grandma didn't believe Mom when she told that her stepdad was molesting her. Mom doesn't want to believe me. Every member of mama's side of the family has the same rule. What happens in this house stays in this house. This level of secrecy must have been started to cover the tracks of the first child molester. Secrets are pedophiles strongest and most powerful weapon. What harm has keeping secrets caused in this family?

Aj turned over her notes and wrote:

KARMA

The grandmother, Virginia, stayed married to a pedophile. She refused to protect or even believe her daughter Mabel. She turned her back to any and everything that threatened her lifestyle. Even when Mabel was groped by her stepfather at the dinner table, in front of witnesses, still Virginia did nothing. Now her daughter Nancy is married to Ron, a child molester who very well may have molested his own daughter Niyah.

How long had Ron groomed Niyah before he got into bed with her? He used to take her to the bathroom and go inside with her even when she was seven years old. When Nia caught them together was it the first time or had she finally worked up the courage to bust into the room after being left on her own time and time again? Ron was prone to stolen moments. What better time to make his pedophilic move than when his wife was in the hospital giving birth to their baby?

Aj told the truth the day after Ron sexually harassed me at Coco's house. Aj told Coco because it happened at her house. Coco twisted my words and swept it under the rug. Whatever Ron did to Coco's daughter Melanie, when she was a little girl left Melanie distraught and in tears.

Coincidentally, of course, after Aj blew the whistle on Ron as a child molester who was stalking her, and after Aj made sure her aunt Nancy caught Ron secretly handing money to only Aj at Buddy's Christmas party, Ron's friendship with Aj's father ended abruptly, after three years. Ron and Nancy stopped by the Rashond house all of the time, that is, until Ron was exposed. Of course, Nancy knows there was more to the story than she was told, why else would they abruptly stop coming by for free meals?

Nancy was never told the truth, or maybe she was, and she and Coco agreed to bury it because there was no penetration, minimize it, and make it go away to save Nancy's marriage. Bully and shame Aj into keeping quiet, keeping the secret as their mother had done to their sister Mabel. Did Nancy not know to protect her daughters from their father? Nia walked in and caught Ron in bed with Niyah. Nancy bullied her daughter into recanting her story.

Niyah has a daughter. The real question is will you trust your father around your daughter once she starts budding into a young lady? Do you want your father to love your daughter the same way he loved you?

When does it stop? Why is this like a generational thing when the simple truth can make it stop? Stop sweeping the truth under the rug. Stop allowing these sick individuals to commit this crime against other family members.

-Tell your truth-

B. T. Books
GET PUBLISHED!
Your voice in print.
www.BTBks.com

Made in the USA
Columbia, SC
08 June 2019